For more than forty years,
Yearling has been the leading name
in classic and award-winning literature
for young readers.

Yearling books feature children's
favorite authors and characters,
providing dynamic stories of adventure,
humor, history, mystery, and fantasy.

Trust Yearling paperbacks to entertain,
inspire, and promote the love of reading
in all children.

D1016361

OTHER YEARLING BOOKS YOU WILL ENJOY

FAST FORWARD: A DANGEROUS SECRET, *Ian Bone*

CHIG AND THE SECOND SPREAD, *Gwenyth Swain*

THE GYPSY GAME, *Zilpha Keatley Snyder*

WITH LOVE FROM SPAIN, MELANIE MARTIN
Carol Weston

BLUBBER, *Judy Blume*

THE UNSEEN, *Zilpha Keatley Snyder*

BOYS AGAINST GIRLS, *Phyllis Reynolds Naylor*

MOLLY MCGINTY HAS A REALLY GOOD DAY
Gary Paulsen

zooman Sam

LOIS LOWRY

Illustrated by Diane deGroat

A YEARLING BOOK

For Bailey,
who loves Sam,
and for Grey,
who will

Published by Yearling, an imprint of Random House Children's Books
a division of Random House, Inc., New York

Visit us on the Web! www.randomhouse.com/kids

Educators and librarians, for a variety of teaching tools, visit us at
www.randomhouse.com/teachers

ISBN: 0-440-41676-0

Reprinted by arrangement with Houghton Mifflin Company

Printed in the United States of America

March 2001

10 9 8

1

"What are you doing, Sam?" his mother called from the bottom of the stairs. "Dinner will be ready soon!"

"Nothing," Sam called back from his bedroom. *Nothing* wasn't exactly true. But it was what you said when it was too hard to describe the truth. The truth would have been "I'm looking at my clothes."

But then his mom would have said, "Why are you looking at your clothes? Is there something wrong with your clothes?" and she would have come up the stairs, and then Sam would have tried to explain *why* he was looking at all his clothes, and his mom would have noticed that he'd made a mess in his closet because when he stood on a chair and pushed the hangers to one side, they all fell down, and now everything was in a heap, and Sam *planned* to pick them all up and hang them again, he just hadn't done it yet, but his mom wouldn't understand that, and she'd probably get mad, and —

It was easier to say "Nothing."

"We're having chicken," his mom called, and he could hear her feet going back to the kitchen. Then he could hear the thumping of dog feet. Sam laughed a little. He knew it was Sleuth, the Krupniks' dog. Like most dogs, Sleuth understood "Come," and "Sit," though he didn't always choose to obey. But unlike most dogs, somehow Sleuth could recognize any word that related to food. And Sam's mom had said "chicken," so Sleuth, who spent most of his time sleeping (and probably dreaming of food), had leaped up to follow Mrs. Krupnik down the hall.

Sam didn't even care about chicken. He was too absorbed in his search. He began to poke through the pile of clothes on the floor of the closet.

He picked up a blue and white sailor suit and made a face. He remembered the wedding at which he had worn it. His sister, Anastasia, had been a bridesmaid, and she wore a beautiful dress. She looked like a princess, or like a Barbie. Sam wouldn't have minded if he could have dressed like a prince, or a Ken. He would have worn a tuxedo. Sam thought tuxedos were cool.

But instead, his mom had made him wear that dumb sailor suit. It had short pants. His mom told him that it made him look like Popeye, and she had even drawn a marking-pen anchor tattoo on his arm, under the sleeve. But it wasn't true, about Popeye. The suit was just a dumb baby sailor suit, and everybody at the wedding said he looked cute. Sam didn't want to look cute. He wanted to look tough and mean. He decided he would never, ever wear the sailor suit again. He rolled it into a ball and threw it into the darkest corner of the closet, next to the folded-up stroller.

Sam noticed his Osh-Kosh overalls hanging from a hook. He stood on the chair and took them down. He liked his overalls. His sister had some just like them, and sometimes he and Anastasia wore their overalls on the same day. Their dad called them Ma and Pa Kettle when they wore their overalls.

Sam liked that. He didn't know who Ma and Pa Kettle were, but he liked the sound of those names.

But today the overalls were not what Sam needed. He thought about climbing up to re-hang them on their hook, but that was too much bother. He rolled them up and threw them into the other corner of the closet, where they settled in a heap on top of his ant farm.

"Five minutes till dinner! Wash your hands, please!"

Hearing his mother's voice, Sam sighed. He looked at the clothes remaining in the pile that had fallen from the rod. Halfheartedly he picked up his bright yellow raincoat and thought about it for a minute. He liked his rain-coat. But today it was not what he needed. He dropped the raincoat on the floor on top of his red snowsuit.

He looked toward the other side of the room, where he had already dumped the clothes he had taken from his bureau drawers. Socks and underpants and T-shirts and sweaters and jeans were strewn across the rug. His Superman paja-mas dangled across the arm of the rocking chair, and a sweatshirt that said HARVARD UNI-

VERSITY had somehow landed on the head of Sam's old rocking horse.

None of the clothes were right. Sam felt like a failure. He felt like the biggest, dumbest poophead in the world. He began to cry. He kicked the side of his bed in frustration, and his cat, who had been sleeping in her usual place beside Sam's teddy bear, woke in surprise. She jumped from the bed with an irritated swish of her tail, gave Sam a disgusted look, and left the room.

That was the final blow. Even his cat hated him. Sam began to cry harder.

"Everybody! Dinner's on the table! Come right now!"

Sam heard his father's chair creak and knew that his dad had pushed himself back from the desk in his study. He heard his dad's heavy footsteps head to the dining room.

He heard the clumping sound of the heavy hiking boots his sister liked to wear, and knew that Anastasia was coming down the stairs from her third-floor bedroom. Then she crossed the hall outside his room, and he heard her boots again as she headed, clumpety clump, down the second flight of stairs.

He smelled chicken.

"Sam! Hurry up!"

Still angry, still crying, Sam surveyed the wreckage of his room. His toes hurt because he had kicked his bed with his bare feet. His cat despised him. His friends would all laugh at him tomorrow. His teacher, Mrs. Bennett, would be nice, he knew, but secretly she would be thinking he was the biggest dumbo in the world.

Sam left his bedroom, slammed the door behind him, and stomped noisily down the stairs. He wailed in despair and frustration.

"Sam," said his mother as he entered the dining room, "what took you so long?" She was serving the chicken and passing the plates. She looked at Sam and blinked in surprise. "My goodness," she said.

"Sam, why are you crying?" asked his father. He was carefully mounding mashed potatoes on each plate that he took from Sam's mom. He looked at Sam and held a whole spoonful of potatoes in midair, forgetting to plunk it onto the plate.

His sister, Anastasia, was just about to dip a spoon into a bowl of peas. Anastasia was always in charge of vegetables, and that was a good thing, because she understood how important it was not to let certain vegetables — like beets, especially beets — touch other things, like potatoes.

But Anastasia, without looking, dropped a whole spoonful of peas onto a plate, right on top of a chicken leg. Some of the peas fell from the plate onto the tablecloth, and no one even noticed.

They were all staring at Sam.

"Why are you *naked?*" Anastasia asked.

2

There was Chunky Monkey ice cream for dessert. That was both good and bad.

It was good because Sam loved Chunky Monkey. It was one of his favorites. So it made him feel pretty happy to have a big bowl of Chunky Monkey in front of him, and a spoon in his hand.

But it was bad because of its name. The name Chunky Monkey reminded Sam of his problem, his whole big problem, which he would never ever be able to solve; and thinking of his unsolvable problem made Sam feel like crying once again, even though he had already stopped crying long enough to eat his chicken.

He had even gotten dressed — well, sort of dressed — before he climbed into his chair to eat his dinner. His mom had taken a big sweatshirt from a hook in the back hall, and dropped it over his head, and rolled up the sleeves. The sweatshirt had a picture of Beethoven on it. Beethoven was a man with a very frowny face, so his picture suited Sam perfectly. Sam was frowning, just like Beethoven.

"I'm going to be the dumbest one in my class," he told his family again.

"Of course you're not, Sam," his mom reassured him. "I wish Mrs. Bennett had let you know sooner, though, about Future Job Day."

"Well," Sam confessed, "she gave us a note to bring home."

"When did she do that?"

"Last week."

"For heaven's sake, Sam," his mother said, "why didn't you show me the note?"

Sam tried to remember what had happened to the folded note from Mrs. Bennett. "I had it in my pocket," he said.

"Yes? And then what? Did it end up in the washing machine?"

"I do that all the time, Sam," Anastasia said. "Usually with dollar bills. They come out of the dryer all wadded up. It's hard to unfold them after they're washed and dried."

"No," Sam said, remembering. "I took it out of my pocket and I tried to fold it into an airplane."

"Why?" His father sounded interested.

"I don't know. I wanted an airplane."

"Well," his mother asked, "what happened to it after you folded it? Where *were* you when you made the airplane?"

"In the carpool car."

"Whose day was it to drive?"

Sam thought. He remembered sitting in the back seat, next to Adam, and next to Adam was Emily, and Emily said that she might throw up, but she didn't. And he remembered that Leah's wheelchair was folded in the way-back part. Leah was in the front seat, next to —

"It was Leah's mom," Sam said.

"So," Mrs. Krupnik said with a sigh, "if I call Leah's mother, and ask her to look in the back seat of her station wagon, there on the floor, along with the crumpled-up McDonald's wrappers —"

"There might not be McDonald's wrappers, Mom," Anastasia said. "Leah's mom might be very neat. She might clean her car every day."

"No, she isn't," Sam said. "She's messy, like

11

you. There's a whole lot of junk on the floor of her car. There's a rawhide bone that Leah's dog put there. And there's a Barbie doll, and —"

"And a note from Mrs. Bennett, folded into an airplane. Darn it, Sam." Mrs. Krupnik sighed again.

"No, there isn't," Sam announced. "I flew it out of the car window, right near the library. It crash-landed in a bush."

Tomorrow was going to be Future Job Day at Sam's nursery school. The children were supposed to come, Mrs. Bennett had explained to them (and to their parents, in a note that had turned into an airplane and crash-landed in a bush), dressed the way they would dress as grown-ups, in whatever job that they hoped to have someday.

Sam didn't really truly know what he wanted to be when he was grown up. Sometimes he thought he wanted to fly an airplane, and sometimes he thought he wanted to be the guy in the diving suit who fed the fish in the big tank at the New England Aquarium.

All he knew for sure was that he wanted to stand in front of the class tomorrow and hear all the children go "Ooooh" when he told about his

Future Job. More than anything Sam didn't want to be ordinary. He had always been *ordinary,* and he was tired of it. What he wanted was to be — well, he had a special name for it, a private name that he would never tell anybody. It meant somebody important, somebody interesting, somebody more than ordinary. Sam called it, just to himself, the Chief of Wonderfulness.

"Leah has a white coat," Sam told his family, "and she's going to wear a stets——, a stetso——"

"A Stetson hat?" asked Sam's dad. "Does Leah want to be a cowgirl?"

"No," Sam said impatiently. "The thing you wear around your neck when you're a doctor. Leah's going to be a doctor."

"Oh," said Mrs. Krupnik, "a stethoscope."

"Yeah," Sam said. "A stetsocope. And Adam's going to be a fireman. He's wearing his raincoat and boots. And maybe his mom will let him bring a hatchet." Sam sighed in envy, thinking about the hatchet. It would be so cool to bring a hatchet to school. It wouldn't make you Chief of Wonderfulness, but it would be very, very cool.

"Well, Sam," his mother suggested, "you could be a fireman, too. You have a yellow raincoat. I think you even have a plastic fireman's hat someplace. No hatchet, though. Sorry about the hatchet."

"No!" Sam wailed. He had already thrown his raincoat on the floor of his closet. Sam didn't *want* to be a fireman. All of the boys were going to be firemen, except for maybe stupid old Josh, who said he was going to be an Indian — and Mrs. Bennett said no, you should say Native American; so Josh said okay, he was going to be a Native American, and he had a feathered headdress to wear.

"Stupid Josh is going to be a Native American," Sam muttered.

"Don't say 'stupid,' Sam," his mother said.

"But, Mom," Anastasia pointed out, "it *is* stupid. You can't be a Native American unless you *are* Native American. That's like saying you've decided to be Italian."

"Stupid old Josh," Sam muttered again.

"I have an idea," Sam's dad said. "Sam, you could wear a necktie. I can lend you one . . ."

Already Sam could tell he was going to hate this idea. But he waited politely for his father to finish.

"And," Myron Krupnik went on, "you can

carry a briefcase. I have an old one you can borrow. We can fill it with papers."

"Why?" Sam asked.

"Ta-da!" his father said proudly. "You'll be a college professor. Just like . . ." He waited expectantly.

"Just like you," Sam said gloomily.

"Dad," Anastasia said, "we love you. But that would not be a cool Future Job for Sam. It's too boring."

Mrs. Krupnik stood up and began to stack the empty plates on top of one another so that she could take them to the kitchen. "Well, Sam," she said. "If you had brought home the note, we would have had more time to prepare. But as it is, you'll have to decide on something, and you'll have to decide on it quickly." She looked at her watch. "It's one hour until your bedtime."

"I already decided," Sam explained angrily, "but I don't have the right clothes."

Everyone else had finished eating dessert, but Sam hadn't even started. He picked up his spoon and put it into his ice cream.

"Well, what did you decide?" his mother asked. "What are you planning to do as a Future Job?"

Sam discovered that his bowl was filled with liquid. Absolutely everything was going wrong for him.

"My Chunky Monkey!" Sam wailed. Just saying the words reminded him, once again, of his Future Job. He had been thinking about it all day. He was pretty certain that it would cause all of the children, even the ones who might have hatchets, to say "Ooooh" when he stood in front of the class. Poking his spoon into the soup that had once been ice cream, he announced it to his family.

"A zookeeper!" Sam said.

3

There were a lot of things that Sam loved about his family.

He loved that they didn't fight, the way Tucker's family did. Sam had been invited once to Tucker's house to play, on a Saturday afternoon, and he had a terrible time. Tucker's dad was raking the yard, and Tucker's mom yelled that he wasn't doing it right, and then he yelled back, and finally he slammed down the rake and said a very bad word, the S-word, and Sam got a stomachache and wanted to go home.

Sam's mom and dad didn't do that. They argued sometimes, but they never yelled the

S-word at each other and made people have stomachaches.

And Sam loved that his family laughed a lot and acted goofy. He sort of hoped that his friends wouldn't be there, noticing, when his mom and dad and sister acted goofy, like the time they all did a ballet in the living room, twirling around on their toes. Maybe friends wouldn't understand that and would think his family was weird.

But Sam loved it when they all acted goofy together, just their family, like maybe holding fake microphones made out of bagels poked onto forks, and singing old Beatles songs. Sam's mom always put on dark glasses and said she was Yoko, even though Yoko wasn't really truly a Beatle. And they always let Sam be Ringo and do the drums.

Sam thought he had been born into the best family in the world. Even times like tonight, when he was howling and crying and telling them that he had an unfixable problem, secretly he knew that his family would be able to help him fix it. So while he was wailing, he was also waiting.

"Stop crying, Sam," his mother said. "Let's figure this out. And here: you can have some fresh ice cream." In his corner in the kitchen they could hear Sleuth leap up eagerly at the words *ice cream*. Sleuth's hearing was phenomenal. He came into the dining room. But no one paid any attention to the dog. Sam's mom spooned some fresh Chunky Monkey into Sam's bowl.

"Are you certain of that choice, Sam?" Mrs. Krupnik asked. "The last time we took you to the zoo, we didn't stay as long as we had planned. Remember? It was in the summer, and it was so hot, and —"

"The only bad thing about a zoo," Sam said, "is the smell. You could get used to it."

"I don't know," his mother said, in a dubious voice. "I'd have a pretty hard time getting used to it, I think. The chimpanzee cage was pretty awful." She licked the spoon she had used to serve the ice cream, but she made a kind of bad-memory face.

"Only the smell," Sam reminded her. "Everything else about the chimpanzees was good."

His mother sighed. "Well, they had cute smiles." She widened her mouth and tried to imitate a chimpanzee smile.

"Show some teeth, Mom," Anastasia said.

Sam's sister made her own chimpanzee smile, with some teeth exposed. "Huh, huh, huh," she said, in a chimpanzee voice.

"You need more lips," Sam's father announced. He'd been reading the *Boston Globe* after dinner, while he sipped his coffee. Sam's mom didn't like people to read at the table, but sometimes she said, "Oh, all right, Myron, just this once." She had said that tonight.

Myron Krupnik put down the *Boston Globe* and did an imitation of a chimpanzee face. He shaped his mouth into a wide smile, and exposed some teeth, but then — this was the best part, Sam thought! — his dad fluffed out his lips. For an instant he looked exactly like a chimpanzee. His beard looked like chimp fur, his mouth looked like a chimp mouth, and his bald head looked like a chimp head.

"Cool!" Sam said.

"Amazing," Mrs. Krupnik said. "If you'd just take your glasses off, Myron —"

"Gross, Dad," Anastasia said. "That was *so* gross."

Sam's dad made his chimp face disappear. He looked like Myron Krupnik again. "It's all in the lips," he explained. He picked up the *Boston Globe* again, and continued reading about the

Patriots for a moment. But then he put the paper down.

"What does a zookeeper wear?" Sam's dad asked. Myron Krupnik knew a lot about almost everything. If you asked Mr. Krupnik how to build a rocket, or why the president of the United States wasn't a woman, he would tell you. But sometimes, like right now, Sam was surprised to find that his father was missing important information. *Everyone* knew what zookeepers wear, Sam was secretly thinking.

But he was wrong. Everybody didn't.

"Jeans," Anastasia said, to Sam's amazement. Even his sister didn't know.

"Yes, I'm quite sure it would be jeans," Sam's mother said. "We won't have any trouble at all, fixing you up as a zookeeper, Sam. You were upset about nothing."

"Not jeans," Sam insisted, and a little Chunky Monkey dribbled out of his mouth. He swallowed. "They wear a special zookeeper suit," he told his family, trying very hard to use a polite and patient voice.

"I'll show you!" Sam said. He put down his spoon, climbed out of his seat, and ran into his father's study. He knew exactly where to look. Mr. Krupnik's study was lined with bookcases.

Most of them held grown-up books, books with no pictures at all, books that Sam had never even opened. But beside the couch, on the lowest shelf, next to the floor, were Sam's books.

He had other books in his own bedroom — a whole shelf full — but his favorites were here in his dad's study, so that in the evening, after dinner, he could curl up in the corner of the couch, next to his dad, or maybe on his lap, while his dad read to him.

Holding up the bottom of his father's big Beethoven sweatshirt so that he wouldn't trip on it, Sam squatted down beside the bookcase and found the book he wanted. He took it back to the table, where his family was waiting.

"I remember that one, Sam," his dad said. "We've read that one lots of times."

Sam placed the book on the table in front of his dad. He stood beside him and watched while his father turned the pages of the zoo book.

"The zookeeper's on the page with the lion," Sam whispered. *"There."* He pointed when his dad reached that page.

Katherine Krupnik, Myron Krupnik, and Anastasia Krupnik all leaned over to examine the zookeeper. Sam didn't need to. Sam knew *exactly* what the zookeeper was wearing.

"Oh, I see, Sam," his mother said. "It *is* a special zookeeper suit. Oh, dear."

"And hat," Sam added, without looking at the picture. The picture was memorized inside his head.

"Yes. And hat. Oh, dear," his mother said a second time. She was frowning. Not like Beethoven, though. Beethoven was frowning a grouchy frown. Katherine Krupnik was frowning a *thinking* sort of frown.

Sam's dad sighed. "I still say a college professor would be a good choice," he said. "A briefcase, maybe a nice striped tie —"

"No," Mrs. Krupnik and Anastasia said together.

"Sam wants to be a zookeeper," Anastasia said.

"I think we can do this," Sam's mom said in a determined voice.

Sam began to finish his Chunky Monkey. His mother and sister were examining the picture carefully.

"I would call it a kind of *coverall,* Sam," his mother said.

"Sometimes garage mechanics wear them," Anastasia added.

"Right!" Sam said. He remembered going to

the garage with his dad, to have the snow tires taken off the car. Sam liked watching when they put the car up high so they could look at its bottom. He wanted to ride in it when it went up, but they wouldn't let him.

At the garage, there was a guy with grease all over his face, and a dirty rag sticking out of his pocket. His sister was right; the suit the garage guy wore was very much like a zookeeper's suit.

"Coverall?" Sam asked.

"Coverall," said Katherine Krupnik. "I think I can do it."

"And the hat?" Sam asked. "The special zookeeper's hat?"

There was a silence. Then Sam's sister, Anastasia, said, "I have an idea about the hat."

What a wonderful family I have, thought Sam.

4

Sam, still wearing his father's huge Beethoven sweatshirt, stood beside the kitchen table. He watched with interest as his mother began to cut with her big scissors. Anastasia had gone to the telephone.

"There!" Mrs. Krupnik held it up. "What do you think?"

Sam scrunched up his face and examined the suit. It had been his last year's winter pajamas: soft, fleecy, gray pajamas that felt cozy and warm on a snowy night.

Mrs. Krupnik had carefully cut off the red striped cuffs at the end of each sleeve. She had cut off the feet. So there was nothing left now but a one-piece gray suit with a zipper up the front.

"I'm going to hem the raggedy edges," she explained. "The places I cut? They'll be nice and neat when I'm finished." She opened the kitchen drawer that contained her sewing things, and began to push a gray thread carefully through the eye of a needle.

"It's pretty good," Sam said.

"Just pretty good? I thought you'd say 'spectacular,' Sam."

"Well," Sam explained, "it needs some words on it. Right here." He pointed to the left side of his chest.

"Words?" his mother asked.

"See?" Sam opened the book to the page with the lion and the zookeeper again. The man in the gray coverall had some writing on the upper left side of his suit. Sam didn't know what it said.

His mother examined it carefully. "Oh," she said. "I see what you mean."

"Two words," Sam pointed out. "But I can't read," he added.

"What's the first letter, Sam?" his mom asked with a smile.

Sam examined the illustration. "Z," he told his mom.

"And what's the sound a Z makes?"

"Zzzzz," Sam said, grinning. He always liked when his mom played the sound-of-letters game with him.

"Next?"

Sam peered at the page. "O," he said. "*Two* O's."

"The sound of two O's?" asked his mom. She had begun to hem the end of a sleeve.

"Ooooooooooo," Sam said.

"Put it together."

"Zoo!" Sam said happily. Then he frowned. "There are more letters," he pointed out.

"What's next?"

"K." He made the sound. "Keh, keh, keh." Without waiting for his mom to prompt him, he added it to "zoo."

"Zook," Sam said. "And then two E's. Eeeeeeee. Zookeeee. And then P."

His mom was busy hemming.

"Zookeep," Sam said. "And more letters, but I don't even need them! It's *zookeeper!*"

His mom smiled at him. She twisted the thread around in her fingers and snipped it off with the scissors. "There. One cuff done."

"There's a whole other word, though," Sam said, "and I don't know what it is."

His mom started on the second sleeve. "Try the letters."

Sam did. The first letter was easy because of Jell-O. "J," he said, and made the sound to himself. "Then A," he went on, under his breath.

Finally, as his mother began on the first leg of his gray coveralls, Sam looked up in delight. "Zookeeper Jake!" he said. "I figured it out!"

"You sure did. Good for you!"

"Can you make letters on my pajamas? I mean my coverall? My zookeeper's suit?"

His mom sighed a big sigh. "I was afraid you'd ask me that. I guess I can, Sam. I'll try, anyway. What color do they have to be?"

Sam examined the page with the picture. "Red," he told her.

His mother looked through the cluttered things in her sewing drawer. Finally she pulled out a small tangled ball of thick red thread. "Embroidery thread!" she said. "Great! I had no idea I had that. I guess fate wanted you to have a prizewinning zookeeper's suit, Sam."

"But don't make it say 'Jake,'" Sam warned her.

"Not to worry," she reassured him. "'Zookeeper Sam,'" his mom announced. "In big red letters, right over your heart. Let me finish the cuffs first, though."

She turned the coverall around to begin on the second leg. She glanced up at the clock on the wall over the refrigerator. "Gosh," she said, "it's late, Sam. You've got to get to bed. I'll have this ready for you in the morning, so you can wear it to school for Future Job Day. I promise."

Sam slid down from his chair at the kitchen table. "Can I wear Beethoven to bed?" he asked. "Like a nightshirt?"

"Sure. Go brush your teeth."

"Okay. But —"

"And go give Daddy a kiss goodnight."

"Okay. But —"

"But what?"

"What about the hat?"

Mrs. Krupnik set the coverall down in her lap. She picked up her coffee cup and took a sip. "Oh dear," she said, frowning again. "The hat."

"Ta-*da!*" It was Anastasia, bounding through the kitchen door. "Sam, it's all set! You'll have a hat. I have to go pick it up."

"Pick it up?" Mrs. Krupnik asked. "Where on earth —"

"Don't worry, Mom. I'll be back in ten minutes. I'm just going over to Steve's house."

"Your boyfriend's house? At this time in the evening?" Mrs. Krupnik looked dubious.

"Mom, he is *not* my boyfriend."

"Is that who you just called? In my day —"

Anastasia groaned. "I know, Mom, in your day, girls never called boys. But it isn't your day anymore.

"And anyway, he lives just down the street, and it's not that late, and" — Anastasia knelt to tie her hiking boot and then headed for the back door.

"What about my hat?" Sam asked loudly.

"Your hat is at Steve's house," Anastasia told him. She was grinning. "Bye. I'll be back in half an hour, Mom. Trust me."

"This family is nuts," Mrs. Krupnik said. "This whole family is nuts. Including me." She folded the coverall, put it next to the red embroidery thread, and stood up. "Come on, Sam. Up to bed."

Sam took her hand, went to kiss his dad goodnight, and then followed his mother up the stairs and into the bathroom. She watched while he brushed his teeth with his Mickey

Mouse toothbrush. She washed his face and hands. Then she examined his neck and his bare feet. "Not too bad," she said. "Don't tell anyone that we skipped your bath tonight, Sam."

"I'm clean," Sam said.

"Right. We're a clean and tidy family, aren't we?" his mother said.

"Yeah," Sam agreed. But the word *tidy* reminded him of something. He couldn't remember exactly what. But *tidy* made him feel a little uncomfortable.

His mom took him to his bedroom and opened the door. She gasped.

Now he remembered. His bedroom was completely covered in clothing. Every bit of clothing that Sam had ever owned, including underwear, Halloween costumes, snowsuits, sailor suits, and swimsuits, was on the floor, on the bed, on the rocking horse, on the lampshade, on the windowsills.

"*Sam!* What the *heck* —" His mom's face was surprised. Well, it was more than surprised. It was puzzled. No, it was more than puzzled. His mom's face was mad. *Really* mad.

"Remember that I'm your very favorite son," Sam said nervously.

"I'm remembering that," Mrs. Krupnik said in a tense voice.

Sam watched his mother's face. He watched her mouth to see what it would say. Maybe it would say, "Sam, sweetie." He liked it when his mom said that.

Instead, her mouth said, "Clean. This. Up. Immediately."

So Sam did. It was the kind of thing a zookeeper had to do now and then, and it was no fun, no fun at all. But his mom helped him, and when they were finished, she kissed him goodnight.

5

Usually Sam needed a little help getting dressed in the morning. Especially with shirts. Especially if the shirt was a turtleneck. If he tried to put a turtleneck shirt on by himself, his head often got stuck and he felt scared, trapped in the dark.

But this morning, when Sam woke up and saw the zookeeper's coverall neatly arranged on the foot of his bed, he didn't even call his mom for help.

Quickly he pulled on some underpants. White ones. Usually Sam preferred his Superman underpants, but he thought probably a zookeeper would wear plain white.

Then socks. He chose gray ones, with a red stripe around the top, because they matched his outfit.

Next he stepped into the gray coverall, poked his arms into the sleeves, and zipped it up. Cool. It was easy to get dressed if you were a zookeeper.

He slipped his feet into his sneakers and pushed the Velcro fasteners closed.

Then Sam went into the bathroom to brush his teeth. Standing on his special stool, he admired himself in the mirror. He combed his hair as flat as possible because he didn't like his curls. Of course it wouldn't matter, as soon as he put on his special zookeeper hat.

Sam didn't know what kind of hair Zookeeper Jake in his book had because the special hat covered his head. Jake might have curls, or straight hair, or he might even be bald. It didn't matter.

Sam leaned forward, balancing against the edge of the sink, to look down at himself in the mirror. He wanted to admire his coverall. His mother had made nice big red letters over his heart the way she had promised.

He tried to read them in the mirror and was startled to find that he couldn't. The letters were all backward. They didn't look right.

Sam scrunched up his eyes and squinted to see if that would help. But it didn't.

He stepped down from the stool and tucked his chin in tight so that he could see his own chest. Now the letters weren't backward, really; but they were upside down.

Sam sighed. He unzipped his coverall and tried to take it off. But his sneakers were too big. His feet wouldn't fit through. He pulled the Velcro fasteners loose, took off his sneakers, and pulled the coverall off of his legs. Now it was wrong side out.

Patiently, sitting on the bathroom floor wearing only his underpants and socks, Sam figured out how to reverse the arms and legs so that everything was going in the correct direction. Finally he held the suit up and examined his mother's red embroidered words.

SAM, he read easily, and smiled.

Above SAM he could see the familiar Z, followed by two O's. But the other letters were wrong. They weren't the letters he had seen in his book.

"Mom!" Sam wailed. He wadded up the coverall and left the bathroom. He could hear his family downstairs, in the kitchen.

"Mom!" he called again, and hurried down the

stairs, carrying the bundled suit under one arm and his sneakers under the other.

Anastasia was just putting her schoolbooks into her backpack by the door. His father, sipping coffee, was reading the newspaper at the kitchen table. His mother, wearing jeans and a blue sweater, was at the sink, rinsing some cereal bowls. They all looked at Sam with surprise when he entered the kitchen.

"You never seem to wear clothes anymore, Sam," his dad said. "You've practically become a nudist."

"What's going on, Sam?" his mother asked. She turned off the water and looked at him curiously.

"Aren't you cold?" Anastasia asked. But Sam shook his head. He had forgotten that he was wearing only underpants. He dropped his sneakers on the floor.

"What does this say?" he asked in a loud voice. His father, mother, and sister all looked as he unfolded the coverall and laid it on the table so that the red letters showed.

"Oh," his mom said, smiling. "Can't you read it?"

"I can read that it doesn't say 'Zookeeper,'" Sam told her, suspiciously.

"You're right. I started stitching the letters in, just the way they were in the book, and I got ZOO, and then, you know what? I started to run out of room. The letters kept getting smaller and smaller and more and more crowded. Anastasia, do you have a pen? Can you show him?"

Anastasia took a marking pen out of her backpack and she wrote on a paper napkin.

ZOOKEEPER

Sam could see that it didn't look very good.

"So," his mother explained, smoothing the coverall with her hand, "I ripped out all the way back to the ZOO. I had to decide what to do. Actually, it was Daddy's idea. See? I spelled —"

"Wait, Katherine, see if he can sound it out," Sam's dad suggested.

So Sam looked carefully at the first letter after ZOO. It was an M. "Mmmmm," he said, making the sound. "Zoom," he said, adding the M to the ZOO.

The next letter was A. He looked at it carefully, trying to put it together with the M. "Maaa," Sam said aloud. "Zooma."

"Now look at the last letter," Anastasia said. She glanced at her watch. "I have to go in a

38

minute. Want a hint? Think of something that begins with 'super.'"

"Superman?" Sam asked. He looked back at the red letters. "Zooman!" he said in amazement. "Zooman Sam!"

"Is that cool, or what?" his sister asked. She wiggled her shoulders into her backpack.

Grinning, Sam poked his legs into the suit, pulled it up over his arms, and zipped the front. It felt good. He put his sneakers back on, and pushed the Velcro fasteners closed again.

"Zooman Sam," he said to himself. He walked around the kitchen, pretending that he was checking the cages. "Here comes Zooman Sam!" he called to the pretend animals.

"Be a lion, please," he instructed his dad.

Myron Krupnik looked up from his newspaper and roared fiercely. Sam carefully put a piece of bacon into his father's open mouth.

"Sleuth?" Sam said. "Bacon?" The dog looked up eagerly. "Be a wildebeest." Sam loved the word *wildebeest.* At the sound of the word *bacon,* Sleuth jumped up and bounded over to where Sam stood. Sam fed him the bacon.

"Giraffe, please," he said to his mother. She stretched her neck silently and leaned down toward Sam. Quickly Sam went to the windowsill where his mother kept small pots of herbs. He pulled off a mint leaf and fed it to the giraffe, who nibbled politely.

Then the giraffe kissed the top of his head. That reminded Sam of something. He turned to his sister, who was just opening the back door.

"Where's my hat?" he asked.

"I have to go to school," Anastasia said.

"You didn't forget my hat, did you?" Sam asked.

"No, I didn't forget. Look in the hall closet. Mom will explain about the hat, Sam. I can't be late. Bye."

Sam looked around the kitchen-zoo, where all of the animals were savoring their feedings. His lion-father licked his lips and turned a page of the paper. His wildebeest-dog stared hopefully at the zookeeper, yearning for a second helping. His giraffe-mom plucked a dead leaf off one of the pots of herbs and sneaked another bite of mint.

Sam headed to the hall closet to see about his hat.

6

Pleased with his costume, excited about how his sister had solved the problem of the zookeeper's hat, Sam sat beside his mother in the car.

"Everybody will wonder why I didn't come in the carpool car," he worried. He frowned, fooled with his seat-belt buckle, and looked at his mom as she drove.

"No, they won't. I called Emily's mother and told her I'd be driving you to school today. Nobody even notices who comes in what car."

"Anyway, Emily's car always smells like throw-up," Sam said, remembering.

"Poor Emily. She gets carsick."

"I don't get carsick," Sam said. He pushed the button that made the window go up and down.

"Don't play with that, Sam," Mrs. Krupnik said. Sam stopped. He looked around for something else to play with. He wished it were raining. Sometimes his mom let him turn on the windshield wipers.

Sam's mother flipped the directional signal and turned the car onto a quiet, tree-lined street. Sam's school was at the end of this street, in the basement of a church.

Sam bent his knees and tried to fold his legs like Buddha. Anastasia had a little Buddha statue in her room, and sometimes she invited Sam to sit with her like Buddha and meditate. Sam didn't know what meditate was. But he liked sitting like Buddha.

It was hard in the car, though, because of the seat belt. He wondered how the real Buddha, who had a very large stomach, managed to wear a seat belt. He wondered if the real Buddha ever wore red sneakers with Velcro, and a coverall that said ZOOMAN.

Probably not, Sam decided. He poked the little button that turned on the seat warmers in wintertime. That would surprise his mother on her way home.

His mom parked in the school parking lot. She got out of the car, helped Sam out from his side, and then she lifted a bulging dark green trash bag from the back seat.

"I can carry it," Sam said.

"You sure?"

"It's not heavy." Sam lifted the bag and headed toward the school entrance.

"Hi, Sam!"

"Hi, Adam!" Sam called to his friend. He could see that Adam was wearing his yellow slicker and a red fireman's hat.

"What're you, a trashman?" Adam called.

Sam smiled but didn't answer.

"Hi, Sam!"

"Hi, Eli!" Sam called. Eli, too, was dressed as a fireman.

"Hi, Zachary! Hi, Peter!" Zachary and Peter were also firemen.

Mrs. Bennett appeared from the coatroom. "Good morning! Can I help you with that, Sam?" she asked. She took the trash bag, set it on the floor, and helped Sam unzip his jacket.

"You're not a fireman, Sam!" Mrs. Bennett

said. "Good for you! We have eleven firemen, and that's quite enough, I think. Even Josh decided to be a fireman instead of a Native American. What does this say on your chest?"

Sam puffed out his chest so that Mrs. Bennett could read the red embroidered words.

"ZOOMAN SAM!" she said. "That's super, Sam. You can tell us all about what a zooman does when it's your turn. Go hang up your jacket now. And where shall we put your equipment? Is that part of your costume?"

Sam nodded. He pointed to the corner behind the piano, and Mrs. Bennett put the large trash bag there, on the floor, where it was out of the way.

Sam's mom waved goodbye to him. Once, when he had just started nursery school, she had always kissed him goodbye. But Sam didn't like her to do that anymore. So now she kissed him goodbye at home, or in the car, but at school she just gave him a little wave. Not a great big flapping-in-the-air wave; Sam didn't want that kind in front of his friends. He liked just a small finger wiggle of a wave; it was sort of a code, one that he and his mom had agreed upon, and it meant "I love you a lot, and I will be waiting at home for you, with a grilled cheese sand-

wich or a hot dog. Have a wonderful morning at school."

Every single boy except Sam was a firefighter.

Two girls, Jessie and Kate, were carrying briefcases, and said they were going to be lawyers like their mothers.

Leah, as she had promised, was wearing a white jacket and a stethoscope, and announced that she was going to be a doctor. In the carrying basket of her wheelchair, Leah had a lot of pill bottles filled with M&M's, but Mrs. Bennett said that no one could have any until snacktime, even if the doctor prescribed them. Leah said also that she might give shots to anybody who behaved badly, but when Mrs. Bennett said, "I don't think so," Leah made a face and said okay, she wouldn't. Sam, who hadn't planned to behave badly, was nonetheless a little relieved. Sam thought Leah's shots would probably have been pretend ones, but he wasn't certain; and he didn't want a shot, pretend or real.

Mrs. Bennett's assistant teachers, Miss Ruth and Ben, helped the children organize themselves in a big circle. Ben, who was called Big Ben because he was very large, let two children sit on his lap every morning; today he gave Lindsay and Josh a turn. Poor Miss Ruth was so thin that her lap was uncomfortable because her knees were pointy. She was sorry about that, so sometimes she let one of the children wear her big sunglasses. Today Leah, in her doctor's uniform, was wearing Miss Ruth's glasses; she had to wrinkle her nose again and again, to keep them from falling off.

Mrs. Bennett looked around with a smile. "Every single one of you came dressed for a Future Job," she said proudly.

"Becky didn't!" one of the firemen called out. Calling out was not good behavior, but sometimes the children did it anyway. Sometimes even Sam did it.

"I did too," Becky said, and pouted. Everybody looked at Becky. She was wearing a denim jumper, a red turtleneck, black tights, and white sneakers. Her hair was pulled back in a ponytail and tied with a piece of blue yarn.

Mrs. Bennett smiled. "Would you stand up, Becky?" she asked.

So Becky stood.

"Would you like to tell the children about your Future Job?" Mrs. Bennett asked. But Becky looked at the floor, pouting still.

47

"Would you like me to give them a hint?" Mrs. Bennett asked.

Becky nodded.

So Mrs. Bennett thought for a minute. "Becky told me what she wanted her Future Job to be," she explained, "and we tried to figure out how she should dress."

Everybody stared at Becky, who was wearing her regular clothes. Even Sam, who was pretty good at figuring things out, was puzzled.

"We decided to ask Miss Ruth for advice," Mrs. Bennett explained.

Everybody was looking at Miss Ruth, who was sitting on the floor with the children. Miss Ruth smiled. Sam was still puzzled. So were the others.

"Miss Ruth," Mrs. Bennett suggested, "why don't you stand up with Becky?"

So the assistant teacher unfolded her legs, rose, and went to stand beside Becky. Miss Ruth was wearing a blue denim jumper, a red turtleneck, black tights, and white sneakers. Her hair, pulled back into a ponytail, was tied with a piece of blue yarn.

Suddenly Sam got it. Even though it was not good behavior, he called out. "Becky's going to be a nursery school teacher!" Sam shouted.

"Assistant," Becky corrected.

"Do you want to tell us a little about what you'll be doing in that job, Becky?"

"Uh, help children do stuff," she said.

"That's right," said Mrs. Bennett. "You'll be a good helper, and — what else?"

"Teacher. I'll teach them to do scissors," Becky said.

"Good for you. Okay, you can sit down now, Becky." Miss Ruth, the assistant, went back over to her place and sat on the floor again, near Sam. Becky continued to stand.

"And paste," she said.

"That's right. We do a lot of pasting in school, don't we? Okay, now —" Mrs. Bennett looked around the circle.

"And pour juice," Becky said.

"Right. Who wants —"

"And take children to the bathroom," Becky said.

Mrs. Bennett looked at the big clock on the wall. "Good for you, Beck. Sit down now."

"And I would drive one of the cars on field trips," Becky said, still standing. "And read stories," she added.

"Sit down!" Adam yelled. "It's time for firemen!"

"And play the piano!" Becky yelled back.

Sam sighed. He wanted to tell about zookeeping. He wanted to open the big bag behind the piano. But he was afraid it was going to be a long wait.

7

Finally. *Finally.*

It was about to be Sam's turn at last.

He could tell that Mrs. Bennett was getting a little impatient. Becky had been crying, over on the time-out chair, for a long time, sometimes so loudly that you could hardly hear the other children telling about their Future Jobs. Finally Big Ben had taken her to the little kitchen for a glass of water and then brought her back, sniffling, and let her sit on his huge lap; and now Becky was okay, just grouchy, and her face looked all messed up from crying.

Becky cried every single day at school, about something, so they were all used to it. But it was boring, listening to her cry. Sam leaned toward her and made a goofy face, to cheer her up, but she buried her own face in Big Ben's shirt and wouldn't look up.

And all of the firemen were mad now. Each of the eleven had wanted to talk about firefighting by themselves, one after another, but Mrs. Bennett said they didn't have time. She had suggested that they all stand together as a group.

"Suppose you all lived in the fire station together," Mrs. Bennett had explained. "You'd be a *team.*"

"I'm not going to stay at a firehouse with dumb Tucker," Adam had said.

"Your boots are stupid anyway," Tucker replied. "Mine are real fireman boots, but yours are just stupid baby rain boots."

"Yeah, my *sister* has boots like that," Zachary said, pointing at Adam's red rubber boots.

"I bet your sister can't *kick* like this," Adam said, and he kicked Zachary hard.

Even Becky, still sulking on Big Ben's lap, looked over with interest. In a moment, all eleven firemen were yelling and punching one another.

Finally Mrs. Bennett went to the piano and played a chord very loudly. "Only firefighters sing," she announced, and she began to play the familiar melody of a fireman song that all the children knew.

Still looking mad, all eleven firemen — Adam, Zachary, Eli, Peter, Josh, Stephen with a PH, Steven with a V, Tucker, Will, Max, and Noah — began to sing. Their voices were grouchy, but they knew the words and the song seemed to cheer them a little.

> *Clang! Clang! Down the street!*
> *Firefighters can't be beat!*
> *Lights are flashing, sirens scream;*
> *All the firemen in a team!*

There was more to the song, other verses about hoses and ladders. But Mrs. Bennett stopped after the first verse and allowed the eleven boys to clang like bells and scream like sirens for a minute. They liked that. Sam felt a little jealous.

But he felt glad when they sat down at last. *Now* would be his turn.

"Who's next?" Mrs. Bennett asked, looking around the circle.

"Me! Me!" Sam was calling out. So were Leah and several other girls.

Learning not to be first every time was the very hardest part of nursery school, Sam thought. He waved his arm in the air.

"Sam?" Mrs. Bennett said, and pointed at him.

Proudly he stood up and walked to the front of the room.

"Sam's wearing pajamas!" Adam shouted. All of the firefighters laughed. Sam thought they were very rude. But he didn't get mad. He just waited, standing silently, until the children were so curious that they became quiet.

"This isn't pajamas," Sam explained. "This is a coverall. And see the special writing?" He pointed to the red letters on the left side of his chest.

Mrs. Bennett leaned over to look closely. She smiled. "Would you like me to read it aloud to the children, Sam?" she asked.

Sam shook his head. "I want to," he said. "But first I have to show them something." He went to the bag behind the piano and took out his book. He turned to the page with the picture of the zookeeper and the lion. He held it up, facing the children. He turned slowly, the way Mrs. Bennett or Miss Ruth or Big Ben did, when they were reading stories, so that each child would have a chance to look at the picture.

All the children peered intently. Leah took off her huge sunglasses so that she could see better.

"This man is wearing a coverall, like me," Sam explained. "His name is Zookeeper Jake."

"My dad read me that book," Emily said.

"*My* dad read me *Officer Buckle and Gloria*," Noah said. "A hundred times."

"*My* dad read me *Miss Nelson Is Missing*," Steven with a V said. "A *thousand* times."

Sam could see why sometimes Mrs. Bennett became a tiny bit impatient. It was hard, being a teacher. "Shhhhh," he said loudly. "We're not talking about that now. We're talking about zookeepers.

"I'm going to be a zookeeper when I grow up," he announced.

He could tell, looking at them, that all eleven firemen were mad because they hadn't thought of zookeeper.

"The guy in the book has a hat," Adam said. "But Sam doesn't. All of us firemen have hats. Don't we?" Adam looked around at the other firemen, and they all nodded. Eleven fireman hats nodded up and down.

"Well," Sam explained, "I'm about to show you my hat."

He went to the big plastic bag. Carefully he reached in and took out the baseball cap that was on top. He looked at it carefully to be certain he had the one he wanted. Then he put it on his head. It was a little large, and made his ears fold over, but Sam didn't care about that.

Wearing the hat, he went and stood in front of the circle of children again.

"That doesn't say 'Zoo!'" Leah called. "Zoo has a Z!"

Sam tried to sound like a teacher. "Correct," he said. "Good for you, Leah. My coverall has a Z. See?" He pointed. "This says 'Zooman Sam.'"

"Zooman Sam! Zooman Sam!" All of the children shouted it, and Sam waited patiently. He liked the sound of so many voices shouting his special name.

"But zoomen, like me, have to take care of lots of different kinds of animals. So we have lots of different hats.

"Who can guess what this hat says? It begins with C."

All of the children were silent, staring at Sam's hat and the letters on it. "Vitamin C?" Max asked, at last.

"Nope," Sam said. "I'll tell you." He took the hat off and looked carefully at its letters. "C," he said. "U. B. S. That spells 'Cubs.' My mom told me."

"Cubs," all of the children repeated.

"I wear this when I take care of cubs. Lion cubs, or bear cubs," Sam explained.

"Cool," Adam said.

"What if you're taking care of something else, though?" Emily asked in a serious voice. "You can't wear a Cubs hat if you're taking care of a hippo, can you?"

Sam was actually glad that she had asked because it gave him a chance to use his teacher voice again. "Good question, Emily," he said. "You're really thinking.

"Let me show you," he said, and he reached into the big green plastic bag.

8

Sam rummaged in the bag. There were so many hats, and most of them had long words that he didn't recognize. His mother had assured him that every one was a different animal, but tonight he would have to ask for her help.

Sam felt so lucky.

He was lucky to have thought of being a zookeeper instead of a fireman.

He was lucky to have a mom who could make him a zooman coverall.

And he was certainly lucky to have a sister who was good at thinking of solutions to problems.

Anastasia's boyfriend, Steve — well, he wasn't

really her boyfriend, and if she heard Sam say "boyfriend," she would yell at him to stop because Steve was just her friend (but if Steve Harvey was her friend, and he was a boy, Sam thought it was okay to call him a boyfriend) —

Anyway, Steve's father, Harry Harvey, was a sportscaster. He was famous, actually, his picture was in the November 1992 *Sports Illustrated,* and Anastasia had it on the bulletin board in her bedroom, even though Steve was *not* her boyfriend.

Steve's father appeared on TV and sometimes in commercials and once or twice he was on talk shows, which Anastasia always taped even though Steve was *not* her boyfriend.

Talk show hosts called him "Harv." Harv had sort of big hair. Some people said it was a wig, but Anastasia didn't think so; she said it was just TV hair, and she didn't like it when other people made wig jokes about Steve's father.

But he *did* have pretty big hair. And for that reason, Anastasia had explained to Sam, he didn't like to wear hats. They caused him to have hat hair and made him feel ugly. But people always gave him hats. Managers and coaches and players gave him their team hats. He always said thank you politely, and sometimes he posed for a quick photograph, wearing the hat, but then he brought it home, to his house just down the street from the Krupniks' house, and he threw the hat into a closet.

Anastasia said that the closet was *filled* with hats. It was like a hat store, except it was messy and didn't have a cash register.

Her friend who was not her boyfriend, Steve, had set aside the hats that said things like PISTONS and REDSKINS and SUNS. He picked out just the hats with animal names on them, and given them, every single one, a whole trash bag full, to Zooman Sam.

Sam felt so lucky.

Finally he found the hat that he wanted, the one that said TIGERS. It had a picture of a small orange-and-black-striped tiger head, growling, so it was easy to identify. He removed his Cubs hat, placed it in the bag, fitted the Tigers hat on his head, and went again to the front of the circle. He noticed that Mrs. Bennett was starting to arrange scissors and paper on the worktables.

"Mrs. Bennett," he said politely, "I don't think we'll have time for Handwork this morning."

She smiled, and set some blue plastic scissors beside a sheet of orange construction paper. "We're going to be cutting out pumpkins today," she said. "Because a special holiday is coming. Who knows what holiday?"

"Halloween!" all of the children called.

"Mrs. Bennett," Sam said in a louder, but still polite, voice. "I still have a *lot* of Future Job show-and-tell to do."

She put a pair of red plastic scissors and a sheet of orange paper at the next place on the table. She looked at Sam. "I see you've changed your hat," she said.

"Yes. Now I have —" Sam stopped. He remembered that he was supposed to be teaching the children about a zookeeper's job. He turned to the circle and used his teacher's voice again. "Class," Sam said, "you can see that now I have changed to my Tigers hat. A zookeeper has to take care of tigers, too."

Several of the firemen made their hands into claws and began to growl and roar. Becky, still in Big Ben's lap, began to whimper, when Tucker threatened her with a claw-hand.

"Correct," Sam said loudly, over the noise. "Tigers can be very dangerous. Zookeepers have special training. They get to carry guns."

"Where?" Peter called. "Where's your gun?"

"Lemme see your gun, Sam!" yelled Adam.

Mrs. Bennett glanced over. She was putting yellow scissors on a piece of orange paper. "No guns," she said sternly. "Remember the rule? No guns in school, not even toy ones."

"I didn't bring my gun," Sam explained. "But usually I carry it in a holster on my coverall."

"*Cool,*" Adam said.

"Yeah. *Way cool,*" Peter agreed.

Sam was aware that now all of the children were listening with interest. He liked the feeling of being the most important one in the room. It was almost the feeling that he dreamed of: the Chief of Wonderfulness feeling. But he noticed that Mrs. Bennett had finished distributing the scissors and papers and was waiting. In a minute, Sam knew, pumpkins would be more interesting than zoomen.

"I have to train the tigers not to attack," Sam announced. "I use a whip."

All of the children stared. "A *whip,*" he heard them murmur.

Mrs. Bennett came to the circle and stood beside Sam. She put her arm around him. Usually Sam liked it when Mrs. Bennett put her arm around him because it made him feel very special. But this morning he wished she wouldn't, because he knew it meant that she was going to start talking about pumpkins.

Sure enough. "Class," Mrs. Bennett said, "we're already running a little late, and some people haven't had a turn. So we'll go to our tables now and work with scissors to make our Halloween decorations — all these big orange pumpkins — and then at snacktime, we'll talk about the other Future Jobs. I know Doctor Leah wants to give out her pills at snacktime, don't you, Leah?"

Leah nodded happily, and shook the box that contained M&M's so that it made a rattling sound.

"If zoo animals get sick," Sam said loudly, "I have to give them pills. Special animal pills."

But the children weren't listening anymore. They were all on their feet, heading to the work-tables.

"Mrs. Bennett," Sam said unhappily, "I have other animals to tell about." He tilted his head, looking up to see his teacher's face. The Tigers cap was much too large, and made it hard for him to see.

Mrs. Bennett adjusted his hat a little. She glanced over at the large trash bag behind the piano. "How many do you have, Sam?" she asked.

Sam and his mom had counted them that morning, in the kitchen. "Thirty," Sam said.

Mrs. Bennett sighed. He could see her thinking. At the first table, Becky was starting to cry because she'd already cut her orange paper wrong. Miss Ruth was trying to comfort her, but Becky wanted Mrs. Bennett.

"Tell you what, Sam," she said, leading him to his place at one of the tables. "You've done two. Cubs and tigers. Why don't you wear one hat each day, and tell us about one animal each day? You have twenty-eight more. That's almost six weeks of animals!"

Sam brightened. For six weeks he could stand in front of the circle and feel that feeling of being the most interesting person in the room.

"Okay," he agreed. He sat down in the small chair that Mrs. Bennett had pulled out for him. He picked up his scissors and looked around at the other children, each of them carefully cutting orange paper. Sam made a small starting snip.

"Tigers are sort of the same color as pumpkins," Sam announced to his friends.

"Yeah," Eli said. "And with big giant teeth. I'm going to make big tiger teeth in my pumpkin."

Sam ran his tongue over his own small teeth. He cut meticulously around the side of his circle. He thought about teeth, how interesting they were, and about all of the hats he had left.

"Speaking of teeth," Sam announced to the table, "tomorrow I'm going to talk about gators."

The other children at the table stared at him. "Gators?" repeated Becky, in her beginning-to-be-a-crybaby voice. *"Alligators?"* she asked. She put her half-finished pumpkin down.

"Yes," Sam told her. "But don't be scared. I'm going to tell about how zookeepers capture alligators. And how we wrestle them. And how —"

Sam noticed that none of the children at his table were cutting out pumpkins anymore. He noticed, too, that Mrs. Bennett was looking over with a small warning frown on her face.

"Children," Sam said, in his stern but kindly teacher voice, "let's get back to work now. Let's pay attention to our pumpkins."

9

"Don't you want to change your clothes, Sam?" Mrs. Krupnik asked. She was folding clean laundry on the kitchen table. "Here. How about this?" She held up a pair of denim Osh-Kosh overalls.

Sam shook his head. "I'm going to wear my zooman suit all the time."

"All the time? Even to bed?" His mom laughed.

"No, I'll wear my stars-and-planets pajamas to bed. But I have to wear my zooman suit every day because that's what zookeepers do."

"And the hat, too?"

"I have to wear a different hat each day," Sam explained. "But maybe I don't have to wear it at home." He shook his head inside the Tigers cap. He had discovered quite by accident that if he shook his head fast, sometimes the cap, because it was so large, wouldn't shake. The cap would continue pointing straight ahead even though Sam's head was turned to the side. It was a very interesting phenomenon, Sam thought. But it wasn't very comfortable.

For now, he took the Tigers hat off. He could see better with it off. At school, his paper pumpkin had been a little lopsided because he hadn't been able to see well while cutting.

His mother finished folding the underwear and lined everything up neatly in piles; then she put it all into the straw laundry basket and carried it upstairs. Sam followed her.

"I'll make us each a you-know-what in a minute," she said, as she put the folded towels on shelves in a hall closet.

"What's a you-know-what?" Sam asked.

"I don't want to say it because of the dog," his mom explained.

"He's asleep in the kitchen," Sam pointed out. "He can't hear you."

"Well, I meant sandwich. I'll make us each a sandwich."

They heard a crash downstairs. Sam's mom

groaned. "Here he comes," she said. "And he knocked over the wastebasket on his way. What on earth are we going to do about this dog?"

Sure enough, Sleuth came bounding up the stairs. From a deep sleep in a corner of the kitchen, half a house away, Sleuth had heard the word *sandwich.*

Sam scratched the dog behind one ear. Sleuth wiggled his behind happily.

"We have to talk in code," Sam suggested to his mother. "No food words."

"Well, I was about to ask if you would like a you-know-what."

Sam knew what. "What kind of you-know-what?" he asked. "Not the kind I hate, that comes in a can with a picture of a mermaid on it."

"No, not that kind," his mom replied. She knew he meant tuna fish. She also knew that Sam hated tuna fish. "I was thinking of the kind that . . ." She thought for a minute, figuring out how to say it in code. Sleuth watched her. So did Sam.

"The kind that comes chunky or smooth?" Sam suggested.

"Yes, that's it."

"Yes, I'd like a chunky you-know-what," Sam

said, "with, ah . . ." Now *he* was trying to come up with a code word.

"Begins with J?" his mom asked.

"Right. Begins with J. That's what I want for lunch." Sam followed his mom as she carried the laundry basket down the hall. Sleuth ambled along behind, listening to their conversation.

"Mom?" Sam asked.

"What?" his mother asked. She turned into Sam's bedroom.

"Tell me how to spell *Gators*," Sam said.

Mrs. Krupnik opened the top drawer of Sam's bureau and stacked his socks and underwear inside. "G," she said. "It makes the sound of 'guh.'"

"Then A, of course," his mother said. Sam followed her down the hall toward his parents' bedroom. "You can hear the A."

"Gaaaators," Sam said to himself. "Yes," he said. "I can hear the A."

He watched as his mother put his dad's undies away. "Your father is a messy guy," she said. "Look at this. His socks are all in a big jumble." She shook her head the way she sometimes shook it when she looked at Sam's room with toys all over the floor.

"*Jumble* has a J," Sam announced. "I always know J because of Jell-O. Oh, no!" He clapped his hand in front of his mouth. "I said a food word!"

They both looked at Sleuth warily. But he hadn't reacted. Sleuth didn't like Jello-O.

"That's true. Jumble has a J. Let me see, now. Look: he has a green sock matched up with a brown." Mrs. Krupnik sighed and began to re-arrange Sam's dad's socks.

"T comes next," Sam said suddenly.

"Tea comes next? You don't even like tea, Sam. I was going to give you chocolate milk with your sandwich. Oh, *no!* Now *I* did it! *Down,* Sleuth!"

Gradually they calmed the dog, who had be-gun to leap around the room at the sound of "sandwich."

"No," Sam said, when Sleuth had finally re-laxed, "I meant T comes next in *Gator!* After the A! I can hear it! Listen: GaaaaTTTTTor!"

His mom began to laugh. "You sound like a cheerleader, Sam. Gaaaatttor! Gaaaatttor!"

Sam hurried down the stairs and back into the kitchen. The big green plastic bag was still on the floor beside the back door, where he had set it down when he got home from school.

Sleuth followed him, turned around in a circle, and lay down on his folded rug in the corner. Sleuth knew that Sam often slipped him a few treats during lunch. Bread crusts, usually. Sam didn't like the crust. But Sleuth did.

"Right now I'm looking for my hat," Sam explained to the dog.

When Mrs. Krupnik returned to the kitchen with the empty laundry basket, she found Sam waiting in his special chair at the table. His head was tilted back so that he could see from below the bill of the huge Gators cap. Only the tip of his nose and his mouth showed. His mouth had a huge smile.

"I found it all by myself," Sam said, "because I knew the letters."

"Would you like to take a walk over to the Harveys' house, Sam?" Anastasia asked. It was late afternoon, and his sister had come home from school and dropped her books on the hall table.

"Why?" Sam asked.

"Well, you could say thank you to Mr. Harvey for the hats."

"Didn't you say thank you when you went and got them?" Sam asked.

"Of course I did. But you should, too. And I

72

know he's home now. He's flying to San Francisco tomorrow, but today he was going to rake the leaves in their yard. He told me that last night when I picked up the hats. And I saw him out there when I came in from school."

Sam went to the living room window and peered out. Down the street, on the other side, in the front yard of a large brick house, he could see the sportscaster raking leaves. Working beside him was his teenage son.

"Steve is helping him," Sam told his sister.

"Oh?" Anastasia said. "I didn't notice."

"Steve's wearing a dumb yellow sweater," Sam said. He turned his Gators hat around on his head so that he could press his nose against the window glass.

"He is not," Anastasia said defensively. "It's cashmere. I think he got it for his birthday. And it really looks nice with his eyes. His eyes have kind of yellow flecks in them."

Sam wondered what flecks were. It sounded painful, having yellow ones in your eyes. He breathed lightly on the glass. Then he made a mark with his finger on the fogged place. "G," Sam wrote, for Gators. He moved slightly to the left, breathed on the glass again, and wrote, "A."

"Come on, Sam," Anastasia said. "Let's walk over there while they're still outside."

"You just want to see Steve," Sam said. "What are flecks, anyway?"

"I do not. Steve is completely irrelevant to me. I just want you to exhibit some manners. It's very important to learn to say thank you for things."

Sam knew that. Sam had learned to say thank you when he was one year old. He fogged another section of window glass and wrote "T" with his finger.

"Mr. Harvey ought to see how great that hat looks on you, Sam," Anastasia suggested.

"Oh, all right." Sam smeared the places on the window, to erase the letters. He turned his hat back around, tilted his head so that he could see, and followed his sister through the front door.

"Don't say anything stupid," Anastasia whispered to him as she took his hand and led him across the street. Sam liked the feel of the dead leaves whooshing around his feet in the gutter.

"I won't." Sam didn't know what she was talking about. Why would he say something stupid?

They approached the large brick house, and

Sam could hear the scraping sound of the rakes in the yard.

"Say hello," Anastasia whispered. She poked him in the back. His sister was acting very weird, Sam thought. He tilted his head back as far as he could, so that he could look up and see Mr. Harvey's face.

"Hello," Sam said loudly. "I came to say thank you for the hats."

The sportscaster squatted in front of him. "You look great, Sam. It's a little big, but it looks good on you." He straightened the hat a bit on Sam's head. "I'm glad we could find a good use for all those hats."

"What does it say on your suit, Sam?" Steve asked. He knelt beside his dad and looked at Sam's coverall. "Zooman Sam," he read. *"Cool."*

"Tomorrow at school I tell about gators," Sam explained. "Today I did cubs and tigers."

"The Gators are two and one," Mr. Harvey said. He sounded just the way he did when he talked on TV about teams. He was using his "Harv" voice. "Their best running back is out with an injury, though."

Sam smiled politely. He didn't know what Mr. Harvey was talking about.

Anastasia poked him in the back again. He couldn't figure out why she kept doing that. He tried to think of something to say to the Harveys.

"I like your sweater," he said, finally, tilting his head back to look at Steve. "It looks really nice with your flecks."

Before he knew what had happened, Sam found himself heading home. Anastasia was practically dragging him by one arm. "I'm humiliated," she muttered.

"Why? What did I do wrong?"

"You wouldn't understand," his sister said angrily.

And that was true. Sam didn't understand at all.

10

"That dog is getting worse and worse," Mrs. Krupnik said at dinner.

"It's because he's smart," Anastasia pointed out. "Most dogs don't even get it when you're talking about food."

"Speaking of food, there are plenty of seconds here. Does anybody want any more meatlo ——" Sam's dad began to say.

"Don't!" Mrs. Krupnik, Anastasia, and Sam all interrupted him in loud voices. Myron Krupnik was so startled that he almost dropped his fork.

They all waited, but it was okay. Sleuth was in the basement now, locked away, exiled, because he had already disrupted dinner three times, leaping eagerly into the room at the sound of a food word. They could hear him making sad noises, little whimpers and moans, on the basement stairs.

"It's not fair, to keep a dog locked up, separate from his family," Mrs. Krupnik said, "but I don't know what else to do."

"I think we should consider giving him away," Sam's dad said. He poured some gravy over a slice of meatloaf on his plate. "I'm fond of him. But he's driving us all crazy."

"I drive you crazy, too," Sam pointed out, "but you never think about giving *me* away."

"Me too," Anastasia said. "I drive you crazy, too. But you never —"

"Actually," Mrs. Krupnik said, "I think about it quite often. At least three times a week. That time when you borrowed my leather jacket, Anastasia, without asking me, and then —"

"Do we have to discuss this? Isn't this water over the dam? Or under the bridge?" Anastasia passed her plate to her dad, for more meatloaf.

"It's more like one very expensive leather jacket over the dam, or under the bridge, or maybe in the dressing room at T. J. Maxx, or could it possibly be at McDonald's, or wherever you might have left it?"

"I don't see what this has to do with the dog," Anastasia said. "And I don't think we should give the dog away. I love the dog."

"Me too," said Sam. "I love Sleuthie."

His mother sighed. "We all love him. But we haven't done a good enough job of training him. What we need is an animal trainer."

Suddenly everyone was looking at Sam. They were looking at his coverall. They were looking at the red letters on his chest, the letters that said ZOOMAN SAM.

"Me?" Sam said.

His father, mother, and sister all nodded. "You," they said.

At show-and-tell time the next morning at Sam's school, all of the firefighters were wearing their normal clothes. So they didn't have as much to fight about.

Leah had told them about being a doctor during snacktime the day before, and had distributed her M&M pills.

Now Lindsay had a turn. Wearing jeans and a sweater, Lindsay simply held a doll, rocking it gently, and announced that her Future Job was to be a mom. Adam called out that being a mom wasn't a real job, so Mrs. Bennett told them all what an important job it was, and then she read them a book about moms while Lindsay rocked the doll and patted its back.

All of the children listened carefully to the story and looked at the pictures when Mrs. Bennett held up the book. On each page, they saw a different kind of mother doing something. They saw a Japanese mother carrying her baby on her back.

"Yeah," Adam called out, "but that's not a *job!* Nobody *pays* her to do that!"

Mrs. Bennett looked at Adam with a very warning kind of look. Then she read the next page and showed a picture of an African mother bathing her baby at the edge of a river. She and the baby were both smiling.

"What kind of job is that?" Adam called out. "That baby's going to get eaten by an alligator!"

Becky began to cry. Miss Ruth picked up Becky and comforted her.

Big Ben picked up Adam and held him very firmly on his big lap. It was a warning kind of hold.

"Mrs. Bennett?" Sam held up his hand politely.

"Yes, Sam? Do you want to say something about moms?"

Sam nodded. "I want to say that they don't have alligators in Africa."

"We're talking about moms now, Sam," Mrs. Bennett reminded him.

"I know. But I want to say that they have crocodiles in Africa, not alligators."

Becky began to howl. "Crocodiles!" she wailed. "I'm scared of crocodiles!"

"And," Sam went on, before Mrs. Bennett could interrupt him, "I think it's a very important job for that mom to protect her baby from crocodiles."

"That's true, Sam," Mrs. Bennett said. "Thank you."

"But it's not a *real* job," Adam said loudly.

Lindsay continued to stand in front of the circle, rocking her doll. Mrs. Bennett turned a page and showed a picture of an Eskimo mother smearing grease on her baby as he lay on a pile of what looked like bearskins. Sam thought it looked a little yucky and was very glad he wasn't an Eskimo.

Page after page, they looked at mothers caring for their babies. Sam decided that Mrs. Bennett was right. Being a mom *was* a hard job. Not all that much different from being a zookeeper, actually.

"Okay, Lindsay, thank you," Mrs. Bennett said. "Now, let's see. We have just a few people left. Jessica and Kate, would you like to tell us about being lawyers, like your mothers?"

Jessica and Kate carried their briefcases to the front of the circle. They stood side by side.

"You stink!" Jessica said to Kate.

"You stink double!" Kate replied.

"I'm going to put you in jail!" Jessica said.

"I'm going to put you in the electric chair!" Kate said.

Then they went back to their seats in the circle. "That's what lawyers do," Kate explained.

"Cool," Adam said loudly. "I want to be a lawyer."

"Anybody else? Emily? You haven't had a turn, have you?"

"I changed my mind," Emily said. "I was going to be a nun, but now I'm going to be a mom, like Lindsay."

"Well," Mrs. Bennett said, "that's quite a change. But I'm glad you saw what an important job being a mom is, Emily. Okay, class! That's it for Future Jobs. Now we have to get to work pasting some faces on those wonderful big pumpkins we made yesterday."

"Mrs. Bennett! Mrs. Bennett!" Sam waved his arm in the air. "You forgot!"

"What did I forget, Sam?" Mrs. Bennett had moved to the supply closet and was taking out a big jar of paste. Sam saw Miss Ruth move into position near Emily. If someone didn't keep an eye on her, Emily liked to eat the paste.

"I'm going to do a different animal each day, remember? For twenty-eight days?"

Mrs. Bennett sighed. "How could I have forgotten that, Sam?" she said. "Especially when you're wearing that hat?"

Sam adjusted his hat. "Gators," he said.

"Children," Mrs. Bennett announced, "while we do our pumpkin faces, Sam is going to tell us about alligators."

"Alligators!" Becky wailed. "Oh, no! I'm scared of alligators!"

11

At home, that afternoon, Sam replaced Gators in the bag and looked through all the hats that he had not yet worn. He had to choose one for tomorrow.

There were seven caps with words that began with B. Sam knew the sound of B, and he said it to himself, sitting on the living room floor with the trash bag opened and the caps strewn all around him.

"Buh, Buh, Buh," Sam said, and looked at the seven caps with B. Some were long words, just too hard.

But one had two L's, and Sam knew the sound of two L's because there were two L's in *Jell-O*.

The hat also had a little picture, which helped, of a snorting bull. *Bull,* Sam said to himself. If the word *Bull* had an O on the end, he figured out, it would be *Bull-O.* He laughed, thinking about that.

"What are you giggling about, Sam?" his mom called. She was at work in her studio. Mrs. Krupnik was an artist who made the pictures for children's books. He could see her through the open door as she sat on the stool by the special table where she worked on book illustrations.

"Nothing," he called back. It was too complicated to explain. He put on the Bulls cap and arranged his ears inside.

He went into the studio and stood beside his mom. "Tomorrow, at school, I'm doing bulls," he explained. "I did gators today, but it made Becky cry."

"I wish those caps were smaller," Mrs. Krupnik said. She tilted the visor a little and looked at Sam. "I can hardly see your face."

"Probably after I talk about bulls, Mrs. Bennett will read *Ferdinand,*" Sam told his mom.

"One of our favorites," she said, smiling.

That was true. They even had a tape of *Ferdinand* which they often played in the car. Sam and his mother knew the whole story by heart. Sometimes they said it along with the tape.

"But then she'll have to explain about bull-fighting, and Becky will cry," Sam said glumly. "Becky *always* cries."

"Oh, dear," Mrs. Krupnik said sympathetically. She dipped her tiny brush into some green paint and added a bit of green to the picture of elves she was working on. The elves were funny, Sam thought. They had chubby pink cheeks and pointed shoes.

"Nobody did artist for Future Job," Sam told her.

Secretly, Sam wished he had chosen artist. He could have worn jeans, the way his mother did, and put a paintbrush behind one ear, the way she had a paintbrush right now. He could have worn one of his father's old shirts, the way his mother did, and splattered it with paint of all colors.

"People change their minds about jobs," his mother told him. She looked carefully at the green that she had just painted onto an elf hat. Then, while Sam watched, she mixed a little yellow into her green and redid the pointed end of the tiny hat.

"Some kids might want to be, oh, law-yers," she said. "And maybe they even become lawyers — but then they could change their mind and become artists."

"Or they could be zookeepers, and then change their mind," Sam suggested.

"I suppose so." His mother smiled at him. "But not when they have a great zooman suit made by their mom." She reached down and gave him a little tickle. Then she looked at his suit more closely. "Remind me to wash that tonight," she said. "You've been wearing it for two days. That looks like ketchup on the sleeve — oh, no!" She cringed.

"You shouldn't have said 'ketchup,' Mom," Sam pointed out needlessly, as Sleuth bounded into the room. Mrs. Krupnik held the edges of her table tightly so that the dog wouldn't bump into it and spill her water and paints.

"Sam, do me a favor. Take the dog and go practice a little animal training."

"Do I have a dog hat?" Sam asked.

Mrs. Krupnik thought. She had read all the hats to him on the first morning. "No," she said, "I'm afraid not. But you know what, Sam? You have a Timberwolves hat. And a timber

wolf is very closely related to a dog, don't you think?"

Sam thought about it. In his mind he pictured a wolf. There were a lot of books with wolf pictures in them: *Red Riding Hood,* for one, and *The Three Little Pigs.*

He looked at Sleuth, who was very shaggy, with white hair in his eyes and a fluffy tail that curled up over his back when he was happy, and hung down like a snowy pine tree branch when he was sad. Right now Sleuth's tail was up because he was the center of attention.

"Well," said Sam dubiously. "I guess he's sort of wolfy."

"So switch hats and take Sleuth out in the yard for some training. I have to get this picture done."

"Can Anastasia help me?"

"She isn't home," his mother explained. "She had to stay after school for Chorus."

Sam sighed. He headed back toward the living room. He wasn't looking forward to searching through all those hats again. "Come on, Sleuth," he said, and the dog followed him amiably.

"It will begin with T, and it will be the very longest word you have," his mother called.

That made it easy. There were only two T's,

and one was the Tigers hat that Sam had already worn. Sam set his Bulls cap aside and put on the Timberwolves cap.

He took his dog out into the large yard beside the house, and stood there wondering how on earth one went about teaching good behavior to an animal. Sleuth sat cheerfully at Sam's side and pawed at an acorn in the grass.

"Hey, Zooman!"

Sam looked up. Steve Harvey, Anastasia's friend who was absolutely not her boyfriend, was leaning on the gate to the yard.

"Hi," Sam said.

"Is your sister around?"

"No, she had to stay at school for Chorus."

"What're you doing?" Steve came through the gate and into the yard. He scratched Sleuth behind the ear. "Hi, Sleuth," he said.

"Animal training," Sam explained. "It's the kind of thing a zooman has to do."

"Sit, Sleuth," Steve said. Sleuth sat abruptly and looked up.

"Down, Sleuth," Steve said. Sleuth wiggled himself into a lying-down position and looked up through his fringe of hair.

"He's already trained, Sam," Steve said.

"Yes, but he does a bad thing if you say a food word."

"A food word?" Steve asked with a puzzled look.

"Yes. The name of a food. Almost any food. Try it," Sam said.

Steve looked at Sleuth, who was still obediently lying on the grass. He thought. "Cheeseburger," Steve said loudly.

Sleuth leaped up, woofed, and threw himself at Steve.

"Down!" Steve shouted. Sleuth reluctantly lay down again.

"What about a food that tastes horrible?" Steve asked Sam.

"Nothing tastes horrible to Sleuth," Sam explained.

"Brussels sprouts!" Steve tried. Sleuth looked up but didn't move.

"Brussels sprouts taste horrible to everybody, even dogs," Steve explained. Sam nodded. Actually, Sam kind of liked Brussels sprouts. He liked the way they looked like little cabbages. And his mom put lots of butter on them, so they tasted good.

But Sleuth did not react to Brussels sprouts.

"Spaghetti!" Steve said. Sleuth leaped forward and almost knocked him down.

"You got a problem here," Steve told Sam.

Duh, Sam thought, but he didn't say it. His mom thought saying "duh" was very rude.

"We need a gun," Steve said. Then he looked at Sam's face, and laughed. "No, Sam," he reassured him. "Not that kind of gun."

12

Sam sank to his knees beside Sleuth. He put his arms around the dog, and Sleuthie licked Sam's face.

"We can't shoot him," Sam said emphatically to Steve. "We love him!"

Steve Harvey laughed. "No, Sam," he explained. "You didn't let me finish." He sat down on the grass beside Sam and the dog.

"You probably know this already, being a zooman," Steve said.

"I'm only a *beginning* zooman," Sam pointed out.

"Well, the thing that animal trainers all know

is that you have to reward good behavior and punish bad behavior."

Sam thought about that. It made sense. "*Moms* do that," he said. "And dads. And teachers." He thought about Mrs. Bennett sending Adam to the time-out chair. And Becky. And Tucker. And Stephen with a PH. Even Sam had to go to the time-out chair occasionally.

"That's right, Sam." Steve scratched Sleuth behind his ear, through the thick white hair. "Now: we need to teach Sleuth that certain behavior isn't acceptable. So we need to think of a way to punish him when he does it."

"A time-out chair," Sam announced. "That's the best way."

But Steve shook his head. "Dogs don't understand time-out chairs. Time-out chairs are a place for humans to sit and think, but dogs don't do that. What we need is a quick *physical* thing: something that will hurt a little, but only for a second."

"Not a gun," Sam said warily. Suddenly he remembered something. It was something that had happened quite recently. "I know!" he said. "Anastasia did it to me! A quick thing that hurt for a second!"

"Your sister? She did something that hurt?" Steve looked surprised.

"Yesterday, when we went to your house to say thank you to your dad for the hats? Every time I said something dumb, Anastasia poked me with her finger. Like this." Sam leaned over and poked Steve hard, in the middle of his back, with his index finger.

Steve jumped. "Ouch!" he said. "I see what you mean. But you didn't say anything dumb, Sam. You said thank you to my dad. That was all."

"But I kept *starting* to say dumb things. And Anastasia kept poking me. I started to say about flecks."

"Flecks?"

"Yes. Anastasia told me that you had beautiful flecks in your eyes. So when we were in your yard, I started to say about the flecks, and she poked me really hard."

Steve was grinning. "Beautiful flecks? Your sister really said that?"

"Yeah. She said that they were the same color as the highlights in your hair. But she would *really* have poked me if I said about highlights."

Steve ran his hand through his thick hair. Sleuth looked up and woofed slightly. "She likes my hair?" Steve asked.

Sam nodded. "So we need to poke Sleuth, huh? When he's bad?"

"What else did she say about my hair?" Steve asked.

"Nothing. That was all." Sam was impatient. He didn't want to talk about hair. He wanted to start training his dog.

"You want a hat?" Sam asked Steve. "I've got my Timberwolves cap, for when I train dogs. I could get you some kind of animal hat."

Steve was patting his hair, still, and arranging it with his hand. "No, I think a hat might mess up my hair. What time is your sister getting home?"

Sam was getting *very* impatient now. He tried to think of a way to bring Steve's attention back to dog training. "She won't be home till late," Sam said. "She's probably going to stop on the way home and have a —" He looked at Sleuth, who was sound asleep on the grass. "A *hamburger*," Sam said loudly.

At the sound of the H-word, Sleuth woke suddenly and jumped up. He pawed at Sam and Steve in excitement.

"Poke him with your finger!" Sam said.

But it was clear that a finger poke would have no effect on a jumping, woofing dog. Steve scolded Sleuth firmly and finally got him back to a sitting position. "We really need a gun, Sam," Steve said, and then, when he saw Sam's face, explained, "I mean a water pistol."

"I'm not allowed to have guns," Sam said sadly. "Not even toy ones." Sam's parents had the same rule as Mrs. Bennett. They didn't even like it when he aimed a stick and said, "Blam." Sometimes Sam secretly made his fingers into guns and shot things that way, but he didn't let his parents see.

Steve was thinking. "How does your mom wash windows?" he asked.

Sam tried to remember. "Well, first she talks about it a lot. Every day she says, 'Those windows are dirty.' Then after she says that for about a hundred days, she finally says, 'Okay, I'm going to do it. Today I'm going to wash the windows.' And then she looks at my dad, but he says he has to go take the car to be repaired. And then she looks at Anastasia, but Anastasia says she has homework. And then she looks at me, and I say, 'I'll help,' but she says I'm too little. So she does it by herself."

"But what does she use to wash them?" Steve asked.

"Rags," Sam said.

"But doesn't she have a squirt bottle of blue stuff?"

Sam nodded.

"Great," Steve said. "That's what we need. Can you borrow that bottle?"

"Okay. But what're we going to do with it?"

"Squirt Sleuth," Steve said.

13

"Bulls" was a hit at school on Thursday. Sam pawed the floor with one foot, indicating how ferocious a bull could sometimes be, and how important it was for a zooman to be brave and alert. Then, as Sam had predicted, Mrs. Bennett read *Ferdinand* to the class. Instead of standing in front of the circle to talk about zookeeping one more time, he adjusted his Bulls cap and sat down to listen to the story. When they read it at home, sometimes his dad pretended to be a matador. He used a towel for a cape, and Anastasia blew a pretend trumpet when Myron the Matador entered the ring.

Becky whimpered, but didn't cry, because Mrs.

Bennett let her be in charge of the flowers. Becky held a bouquet of artificial flowers, and raised one each time the story talked about how beautiful they smelled to Ferdinand.

On Friday, with his zooman coverall newly washed once again, Sam wore his Bears cap. He demonstrated hibernation (Sam was pretty good at snoring) and showed how a zookeeper tiptoes quietly while his bear sleeps. Then Mrs. Bennett read *Blueberries for Sal.*

"We're a pretty good team, Sam," Mrs. Bennett said. "What cap will you wear on Monday?"

Sam thought about the caps he had not yet worn. There were some scary ones that he wasn't eager to wear. But others were easy. "Colts," he decided.

"Good," Mrs. Bennett said. "I have some nice books about horses."

Throughout the weekend, Sam wore his Timberwolves cap and worked with Steve on training Sleuth. They had refilled the Windex bottle with a mixture of vinegar and water. It smelled terrible.

"But it won't hurt him," Steve had explained. "That's the important thing. He won't like it, but it won't hurt him."

They took Sleuth to the yard. Sam's sister sat

on the porch steps to watch. Anastasia had become very interested in dog training.

"Sit," Steve commanded. And Sleuth sat.

Steve arranged the small bottle in his hand, with his finger on the trigger. "Hamburger," he said loudly. Sleuth leaped toward him, and Steve squirted the dog in the face. "No," he said loudly at the same time.

Sleuth yelped and sat back down, looking puzzled. His nose wiggled, trying to make some sense of vinegar.

"Hamburger," Steve said, again, and the same things happened. Sleuth leaped; Steve squirted; Sleuth sat.

"Now you try it, Sam," Steve said, and handed Sam the bottle.

Sam arranged himself in front of the dog, and when he was ready, he said, "Hamburger!" Sleuth leaped. Sam squirted. Sleuth sat.

From where she sat on the steps, Anastasia applauded.

Sam tried again. "Hamburger!" he said loudly. This time, Sleuth got to his feet, hesitated, and then sat back down.

And one more time. Sam said, "Hamburger!" He held the bottle where the dog could see it. Sleuth didn't move.

From the porch steps, where he had gone to sit beside Anastasia, Steve called, "Hamburger!" Sleuth sat very still.

"*Cool,*" Sam said. "We did it! It worked!"

He turned toward the porch, planning to bow theatrically if his sister applauded again. "Yea, Sam!" Anastasia called. "You guys are great dog trainers!"

She turned to Steve. "You want to stay for lunch?" she asked. "We can make sandwiches out of leftover meatloaf."

At the sound of "meatloaf," Sleuth jumped up, knocked Sam over, and dashed to the porch with his ears flapping. He thudded into Anastasia, one eager paw on her shoulder.

Steve stood up with a sigh. "We have more work to do, Sam," he said. "Let me have the squirter."

It was a long process. All weekend they worked. When they got meatloaf under control, they had to start on peanut butter. With peanut butter done, there was still spaghetti.

It was a tiring job, Sam realized, being a zookeeper. His book didn't show the exhausting parts. His book showed Zookeeper Jake smiling while he pushed a wheelbarrow filled with silvery fish to the seal pool. It showed Jake washing an elephant with a hose. In his book, all of the animals looked happy and well behaved. The elephant lifted one ear so that Jake could wash behind it. The seals cheerfully caught the fish that Jake threw. In one picture, a chimp with a huge smile sat very still while Jake brushed his teeth with a special brush.

Also, Jake's suit, the one that said ZOOKEEPER JAKE in red letters on the chest, always seemed to be clean. Sam's suit wasn't. Sam's coverall had muddy paw prints all over it, and egg yolk from breakfast. His mom had washed it at least ten times, but every day it got dirty again. Every night at bedtime, Sam's mom groaned when he took off his zooman suit and she saw how dirty it was. Every night she asked, "Sam, do you think that maybe tomorrow —"

But every night Sam said no. There were twenty-eight more hats. Then there were twenty-seven. And then twenty-six. Sam still had a lot of zooman time left to do.

14

"My goodness, Sam, you're so tall!" Mrs. Bennett said on Friday morning. "You shot up overnight!" Then she looked at him more carefully and began to laugh. "And I can see why!"

Sam laughed, too. He had thought it was pretty funny when he had looked at himself in the mirror at home. He was wearing six hats today, one on top of the other. He had to walk very carefully to keep them all up there without toppling.

He had finished all of the easy animals with short names, earlier that week. Colts on Monday. Then he wore his Rams cap on Tuesday, and talked about how a zookeeper would take care of sheep.

"You have to shear a lot," Sam had explained. "You have to use special scissors." He used plastic scissors to demonstrate, and pretended to remove the fuzzy coat of a stuffed animal. He knew Mrs. Bennett wouldn't like it if he *really* cut. "Shear, shear, shear," Sam said, as he faked cutting. "Then you make a coat out of the wool," he explained.

"How do you make a coat?" Lindsay asked, with her forehead wrinkled up into a puzzled look.

Sam didn't really know. But he said, "Good question, Lindsay." Then he made a guess. "You sew it with a big needle and thread."

Adam called loudly out from the circle without even raising his hand. "Guys don't sew! Only ladies sew!"

"The zookeeper's *wife* makes a coat," Sam said, after he had thought about it for a moment.

"Excuse me, fellows," said Big Ben. "Plenty of guys sew. There's no rule that says only ladies sew. See this button right here?" He pointed to a white button on his denim shirt. "That button

fell off, and I sewed it back myself, just last night."

Everybody was silent for a moment, admiring Big Ben's button. *"Cool,"* Adam said at last.

"Now," said Mrs. Bennett, "I'll read *Sheep in a Jeep.*" She went to the bookcase.

Sam sat down with the other children. "Shhh," he said, because they were still talking about Big Ben's button. He said "Shhh" so that they would quiet down. But he said it for another reason, too. He was noticing that the first letters of "Sheep" on the book Mrs. Bennett was holding made the "Shhh" sound.

"Shhh," he said quietly to himself again, looking at the title of the book.

On Wednesday, Sam had done Lions. Mrs. Bennett let them all practice roaring for a while until it got out of hand and Adam had to go to the time-out chair, where he continued to roar in an angry whisper, while Miss Ruth read a book called *The Lion and the Little Red Bird.*

Thursday was Bucks. It was almost the last of the easy hats with short names. Sharks was still left, but Sam knew that Sharks would cause problems because it was so scary. He was beginning to have a pretty good idea about how he would handle those very scary hats like Sharks, but he wasn't quite ready yet.

So on Thursday he did Bucks, which he explained to the other children meant "men deer."

"I went to a restaurant with my mom and dad and my Uncle Dan," Eli told the class. "And the doors said BUCKS and DOES, and Uncle Dan went to the BUCKS, and it was the bathroom. So then my mom took me, and we went to DOES."

"When my mom takes me to the bathroom in a restaurant," Lindsay said, "we go to LADIES."

Leah waved her hand in the air. "We get to go to HANDICAPPED!" she said. "Because of my wheelchair!"

"Children!" Zooman Sam said impatiently. "We're not having a lesson about bathrooms today. We're supposed to be talking about deer. Who can think of an interesting thing about deer?" He waited, hoping no one would mention Bambi's mother being shot by hunters because he knew it would make Becky cry.

"Antlers!" called Adam, and wiggled his fingers up behind his ears.

Then Mrs. Bennett did a whole science lesson about antlers. Antlers were pretty interesting things, actually, and Sam wished that he had them. He felt the top of his head, reaching under his Bucks cap, to see if perhaps there were some little knobby things starting. That's the way antlers appeared on baby deer; they just popped up one day, as a surprise. Chicken pox had happened that way to Sam, and had not been any fun at all. Sam wondered whether there might be a chance that antlers could happen to a boy. But it wasn't happening to him, so he sighed and pushed his cap back down on his hair.

And on Friday, Sam wore six hats at once.

"Orioles," Mrs. Bennett read, and she removed the first hat carefully while Sam stood in front of the circle of children.

"Ravens," she read next. "Children, be thinking about what these hats have in common. Why did Zooman Sam wear all of these hats together?"

"Cardinals," she read from the third cap. She lifted the Ravens hat off. "Anybody figured it out yet?"

Adam waved his hand. "They're all *hats!*" he suggested loudly.

Mrs. Bennett smiled and shook her head.

"That's not what I'm looking for, Adam," she said. "Think harder." She removed the third cap and revealed the fourth. "Blue Jays!" she read to the class.

"Can anyone guess what the next one might be?" she asked.

"I know! I know!" Leah called, waving her arm in the air.

"Leah? What's your guess?"

Leah wiggled excitedly in her wheelchair, and Sam knew that she had done exactly what he did, so often: raised her hand and said she knew when she *didn't,* really. "Uhhhh," Leah said, thinking aloud. *"Pigs!"* she shouted.

Mrs. Bennett sighed. "You'd better put your thinking cap on, Leah," she said, and she took the fourth hat off of Sam's head. "Seahawks!" she announced.

"And now one more." With a flourish Mrs. Bennett removed the Seahawks cap. *"Raptors!"* she told the class. "Wow! Anybody know what a raptor is?"

No one knew. But Sam did. "I do," Sam said. "Of course, I'm the zooman."

Actually, he hadn't known until that morning. His dad had looked it up in the dictionary at breakfast, while his mom stood at the sink trying to scrape some of yesterday's peanut butter from the sleeve of the zooman suit.

"Tell the class, Sam," Mrs. Bennett suggested.

"A bird of prey," Sam said.

"Of pray? Like 'Now I lay me down to sleep'?" Emily asked. She formed her hands into a saying-your-prayers position.

"No. A different kind of 'prey.' It means it eats other creatures," Sam explained.

"Oh, no!" howled Becky. "Like bunnies?" She climbed into Big Ben's lap and began to sob.

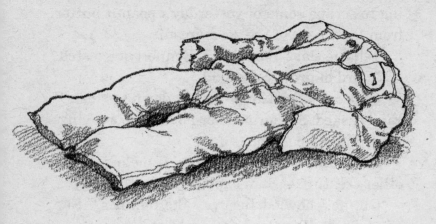

15

Of course the answer that Mrs. Bennett had been looking for was *birds*. Sam's six Friday hats were all the names of birds.

"The zookeeper keeps all the birds in the same place," Sam explained. "Like a big giant cage. It's called a . . ." But he couldn't remember. His father had told him the word that morning, but now he couldn't remember.

"A bird cage!" Adam called out.

Mrs. Bennett leaned down to Sam's ear, the part that showed under the Raptors cap, and whispered the word to him.

"Aviary," Sam announced. "Say it with me, class."

"Aviary," all of the children said, except Adam. Adam said "bird cage" again, and Mrs. Bennett frowned at him and shook her head.

Mrs. Bennett carefully replaced his hats. Orioles, Ravens, Blue Jays, Seahawks, and Cardinals all went one by one back into a tower on top of Raptors, on top of Sam's head.

Sam tried to think of what else he could tell about birds. He didn't find birds as interesting as other animals, and that was why he had worn all six hats at once, so that he wouldn't have to talk about birds on six different mornings.

"When the zookeeper feeds the birds," Sam explained, "he goes into the aviary with his bag of bird food. Then he holds out his hand, with food in it, and the birds come and eat right out of his hand."

"My Uncle Dan has a parrot, and when you hold your hand up, it pecks you," Eli said. "Then it says, 'Only a flesh wound!' and it laughs! It sounds like this." Eli laughed a loud, cackling sort of laugh.

All of the children began to do parrot laughs. Sam tried to capture their attention again. Being a teacher was very, very hard.

"The zooman has to wear thick gloves," he

said, "so that his hands won't get pecked." Then he announced, "Being a zooman is a dangerous job. You have to be very brave."

"Like a firefighter," Adam said. "Probably almost as brave as a firefighter."

"Yeah, firefighters have to be really, really brave," Zachary said in a loud voice. All of the other boys began to nod their heads. One of them began to make a siren sound. Sam saw Mrs. Bennett move to the front of the circle, and he was afraid for a moment that she was going to go to the piano and start the music for the firemen song. But she didn't. She had a book in her hand, and the children became quiet, the way they always did at story time.

"This is a nice one," Mrs. Bennett said, holding up the book, "and it fits right in with Sam's hats because it's about a particular bird. Who can guess what bird?" She held the front of the book so that all of the children could see the cover.

"Owls!" All of the children, including Sam, recognized the book.

"That's right. This book is called *Owl Babies.*"

All of the children got into their listening-to-a-story positions. Three of them — Tucker, Will, and Jessie — put their thumbs into their mouths. Eli and Becky curled up in Big Ben's lap. Leah twirled a piece of her hair around her finger. Josh reached into his pocket and took out the small square of faded wool that he always carried there; it was the last piece of his security blanket, and he held it in his hand during quiet times.

Sam had a listening-to-a-story position, too. He liked to sit with his legs crossed, leaning his head on the big red floor pillow, which was very squishy and soft, with his hands in his pockets feeling the little fuzz that accumulated there.

But a zooman couldn't do any of that, Sam realized. When you were wearing six hats, you couldn't lean anywhere. You had to hold your head very straight. And a zooman coverall had no pockets.

Glumly, Sam sat down on a chair, his posture like a soldier, his chin up so that his head was straight and his tower of hats didn't wobble. He poked at a splotch of egg yolk on the knee of his zooman suit. He listened to the story of the owl babies. The littlest owl baby cried a lot in the story, and felt miserable and wanted his mother. Sam felt a little the same way.

He tried to think about an aviary, and how important he would be, the zooman entering the giant cage wearing his special clothing and carrying special food for all the different kinds of birds, who would be swooping and fluttering and soaring above his head, and —

Oh, *no*. Sam had a terrible thought. He could hear Mrs. Bennett's voice, reading the gentle story of the baby owls in their nest, and he heard her read about the sound of the mother owl's huge wings as she came flying down to care for them. But all Sam could think about was bird poop: how it would come raining down on top of him in an aviary; and even if he was wearing his special hat — or *six* hats, even — he would still be pelted with it, and it would be a million, trillion times worse than a little egg yolk on one knee.

Not for the first time, Sam wished that he had chosen to be a firefighter with all the other boys, instead of a zookeeper, all alone.

16

"Sam, you don't really need to wear all your hats here at home, do you?" his mom asked. "Why don't you take them off for lunch, at least?"

Sam thought about that and decided it would be okay. His head had begun to feel a little weighted from the six hats, and it felt good to put them back into the plastic bag that he now kept in the back hall beside the kitchen.

"I like seeing your hair," his mother told him, and she ran her fingers through it. Then she asked, "You hungry? I fixed some . . ." She hesitated and looked around. Sleuth was in his usual spot in the corner of the kitchen.

Sam could smell what she had prepared for lunch, and he knew it would be safe to say it. "Hot dogs," he announced.

Sleuth opened his eyes, looked up, glanced at Sam, appeared to think for a moment, and to make a decision, and then put his head back down.

"That's absolutely amazing, Sam. In just a week, you and Steve have that dog's behavior under control. What a great animal trainer you are!"

"We haven't finished, though," Sam warned her. "There are some casseroles we haven't done yet. And some desserts."

"Okay, I'll be careful what I say. But here you are: a hot dog." His mom put the plate in front of him. "And after lunch, shall we go to the library?"

Sam loved the library. He had always called it the *liberry,* even though he knew the correct word was *library.* He *liked* saying "liberry," which sounded like "blueberry" or "strawberry" or "raspberry," as if you could make jam out of it, or syrup for pancakes. At the IHOP restaurant, where they went sometimes, there was a little pitcher of blueberry syrup. Sam wondered what it would be like if the chef could make liberry syrup to pour on your pancakes, or liberry jam to have with peanut butter in a sandwich.

When he was older, he decided, he would say the word correctly. But for now, he would say "liberry."

Mrs. Dilahunt, the children's librarian, greeted him when he entered the Children's Room, which was painted in bright colors and had mobiles hanging from the high ceiling. "Hello there, Sam," she said. "My goodness, a different hat today! What does this one say? Let me see." She came out from behind her desk and examined his cap.

"Blue Jays," Mrs. Dilahunt said. "That's a coincidence. Just this morning there was a blue jay on the bird feeder. See over there, at the window?" Sam looked where she pointed, at a feeder filled with sunflower seeds, attached to the sill of the library window.

"When you were here earlier this week, what was it you were wearing? Rams, I think. And last week it was Cubs. You certainly have a lot of different hats, Sam."

"Thirty," Sam told her, with a sigh.

"*Thirty!*" Mrs. Dilahunt said, looking impressed. "I've known only one other person who owned thirty hats, and that was my great-aunt Madeline, who lived in Philadelphia.

"Of course," Mrs. Dilahunt said to Sam's mother, in an amused voice, "my great-aunt Madeline was a complete nut case. I mean *complete.*"

Sam put his stack of books on Mrs. Dilahunt's desk. He was returning the ones that he and his mom had checked out earlier in the week. He had especially liked the one about a boa constrictor named Crictor. Mrs. Bennett had the same book at his school, and he thought she would probably read it next week, when Sam wore his very scary hat that said . . .

Well, Sam didn't want to think about that. His scary hats scared even *him.*

While his mother looked in the grown-up section for her books, Sam wandered over to a low child-size table and looked at the books on display. Mrs. Dilahunt had set all the Halloween books on the table, and Sam sat down in one of the small chairs and looked at pictures of pumpkins and skeletons.

"Don't forget, Sam! Tomorrow morning is 'Saturday Morning at the Movies'!" Mrs. Dilahunt called from her desk.

Sam hadn't forgotten. He loved "Saturday

Morning at the Movies." It wasn't at the movies, actually; it was at the library. Sam had never figured out why she called it "At the Movies" when it was really "At the Library." But he loved it anyway. In the special room with no windows, there was a big-screen TV. He could sit on the carpeted floor. When all of the children were arranged in their places, and nobody was crying or fighting, and everybody was very quiet, Mrs. Dilahunt gave each child a small bag of popcorn. Then she showed a movie. Sam's favorite was *Babe*.

He was afraid, though, that he wouldn't be able to attend this week's movie. Tomorrow he and Steve were going to work on casseroles with Sleuth. Sam hoped Anastasia wouldn't be there. He loved his sister. But if his sister was around when Steve was there, then Steve and Anastasia started laughing about dumb stuff, and nobody paid any attention to Sam. His mom said it was because they were teenagers. She said that Sam would be the same way when he was a teenager, but Sam knew it wasn't true.

Sam leafed through a book about jack-o'-lanterns. He felt a little sad. He remembered a time not very long ago, when he was just an ordinary boy who wore Osh-Kosh overalls and played with his friends and went to see *Babe* at the library. Now, all of a sudden, he had a lot of jobs to do. He had to teach the other children about animals, some of them very scary ones; and he had to train his dog how to behave around the word *lasagna*. He had to wear a suit with not one single pocket and with a grape juice stain — which would not come out in the wash, no matter how hard his mother tried — on the elbow.

And he had to —

But Mrs. Dilahunt interrupted his sad thoughts. "Sam?" she said. Sam looked up.

"I think your mom's almost ready to leave. Have you chosen a book to check out?"

He looked at the jack-o'-lantern book. It didn't look very interesting, actually.

"I picked one out for you," Mrs. Dilahunt told him. "It's really special, as if the author was actually thinking 'Sam Krupnik' when he wrote it. Want to give it a try?"

Sam brightened. "Okay," he said.

But a few minutes later, sitting beside his mother in the car, Sam picked up the book, looked carefully at the cover, and made a little whimpering sound.

"What's wrong, Sam?" his mom asked. She was watching the road as they drove through the shopping area on their way home.

"Mrs. Dilahunt gave me a book, and she said it was special for me. She said the guy who wrote it — what's that called?" he asked his mother.

"The author."

"The Arthur?" Sam said. "He's an aardvark."

"The author," his mother corrected.

"I know," Sam said, "but I like to say 'Arthur.'"

"Why?" Mrs. Krupnik asked.

It was hard to explain. It was like *liberry*. The wrong word just sounded good. "Because he's an aardvark," Sam said.

"Oh," his mom said, though she still looked puzzled.

"Anyway, she said the Arthur probably thought 'Sam Krupnik' when he wrote it. And I thought maybe it would be a book about a boy having adventures, maybe a boy driving a train, or riding a horse, or fighting a giant, but . . ."

Mrs. Krupnik clicked the turn signal and turned the car onto their street. "But it isn't?" she asked sympathetically.

"*No.*"

"What is it about, then?"

"Something dumb. And the Arthur can't even write it right."

"What on earth are you talking about, Sam? You haven't even opened the book yet." His mother pulled the car into their driveway and turned off the motor.

"It's about *zoo hats!*" Sam wailed. "I don't want a book about zoo hats! And look! The Arthur wrote it wrong on the cover!" Sam handed his mother the unopened book.

She looked at it carefully. "Oh, I see what you mean, Sam. It looks very much like zoo hats. But it isn't."

"Because the dumb old Arthur made the Z wrong!"

His mother pulled Sam over onto her lap. He just fit behind the steering wheel. She put her finger on the word that Sam had thought was *Zoo*.

"It's not a Z," Mrs. Krupnik said. "It's a 5. The number 5. On your next birthday, Sam, we'll find a big 5 to put on your cake."

"But what about the O's?" Sam asked, looking at the book title.

"The O's make it say a special number. Two oh oh would be two hundred, and three oh oh would be three hundred, and four oh oh would be —"

"Four hundred," Sam said. He was getting it.

"So this book is called . . ." His mom smiled at him. "Can you guess?"

Sam looked carefully. *"The Five Hundred —"* he said slowly.

"That's right. The title of this book is *The 500 Hats of Bartholomew Cubbins*. And that's why Mrs. Dilahunt chose it for you. She's been noticing all of your hats."

But Sam wasn't listening anymore. He hadn't even listened to the name of Bartholomew Cubbins. Sam had started to cry.

"Five hundred hats!" Sam wailed. He couldn't imagine anything worse.

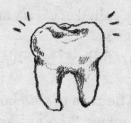

17

Saturday morning was just what Sam had feared. Out in the yard, in their dog-training area next to Sam's sandbox, Steve and Anastasia started fooling around with Sleuth, and the serious work turned into a lot of silliness.

Sam tried using his teacher voice on them. It worked pretty well when he used it at school.

"Children!" he said sternly, looking at his sister and her boyfriend, "I think we're getting a little sidetracked here! Let's pay attention to our task!"

But Anastasia just shrieked with stupid laughter. She squirted the dog-training bottle at Steve and then ran around the yard while he

chased her, trying to get even; Sleuth chased both of them, thinking that it was some sort of game. Sam watched them for a while and tried to figure out why it was that they seemed to be having so much fun when *he* wasn't having any fun at all.

Finally he gave up and went back into the house. He found his mom in the kitchen. The mixer was whirring, and his mom had some batter smears on her nose.

"You licked a bowl, didn't you?" Sam asked in a suspicious voice.

"Sure did," his mother admitted. "Oatmeal cookie batter. Want some? I saved you a little."

That was good news. Oatmeal cookie dough was Sam's favorite, and for a moment he was afraid that his mother had hogged it all, which would have ruined his morning entirely. She handed him a large wooden spoon still covered with gooey batter, and he began to lick.

"I didn't go to 'Saturday Morning at the Movies' because I had to help Steve train Sleuth," Sam said, "but Steve and Anastasia are just fooling around."

"I know," his mother told him. She walked over to the kitchen window and looked out into the yard. Steve and Anastasia were throwing leaves at each other and laughing. Mrs. Krupnik smiled. "That's what being a teenager is like, Sam. When you have a crush on someone, you fool around and act silly. You'll do that someday."

Sam shook his head. He licked the last bit of dough from the sticky spoon. "No," he said sighing. "I'm always going to be sad." He made a very sad face, with his lower lip sticking out, so that his mother could see what he meant.

"My goodness!" she said, looking at his sad face. "Why?"

For a minute, Sam couldn't even remember why he was feeling so sorry for himself. Then he remembered, but he didn't know how to tell about it because it was too complicated. It was about wanting to be the best, the most important, the Chief of Wonderfulness.

Finally, because his mother was waiting, he tried to tell her about some of his sadnesses. "Because I always have to wear a zooman suit," he said at last, "and I don't have any pockets. And I have to wear hats every day. And my ears get folded."

He thought some more. Then he remembered a really big thing. "And I have some very scary animals to do, still."

"Like what?" his mother asked. "You already did lions and tigers. What could be scarier than lions and tigers?"

Sam looked at the floor. "There are five," he told her in a low voice. "But I'm not going to say them."

His mother picked him up. She sat down in a kitchen chair and arranged Sam on her lap. He could smell oatmeal cookies in the oven, and he could hear the clock chime in the hall. His cat wandered into the kitchen, looked around, arched her back, lay down on the dog's folded rug, and began to purr. Sam felt very cozy and comfortable.

"Would you whisper them to me?" his mom asked.

Sam remembered the five hats that he had been dreading. He had placed them in the very bottom of the plastic bag.

He whispered the first one into his mother's ear.

"Gulp," she said. Her eyes opened wide, and she shuddered.

Sam whispered the second.

"Wow," his mom whispered back. "Scary."

Sam whispered the third, and his mom said, "Ooooh."

He told her the fourth, and the fifth.

His mother sat silently for a moment, holding him close. The oven timer made a beeping sound.

"Let me get the cookies out, Sam," she said, "and then we'll decide what to do."

"Okay." Sam climbed down from her lap.

"Want to call Anastasia and Steve? Ask them if they'd like some milk and cookies."

But when Sam went to the kitchen door and called, "Milk and cookies!" it was Sleuth who reacted. He leaped to his feet, knocking over a trash can filled with recyclables, so that cans and bottles fell clattering onto the brick patio; then he thundered to the porch with his ears flapping and his tail wagging, in hopes of a handout.

"Dog trainers!" Sam called in his scolding teacher voice. "You have *not* been doing your best work!"

"Remember when your dad had his wisdom teeth taken out?" Mrs. Krupnik asked Sam. Sam nodded. It hadn't been very long ago. His dad went to the dentist one afternoon, and then he came home with his face all numb and his lips looking a little crooked. That evening, at dinner, his dad ate only soup, and some of it dribbled into his beard. Later, when the numbness went away, his mouth hurt a whole lot. His mom filled a Ziploc bag with crushed ice, and wrapped it in a towel. Then Sam's dad took a pill and lay on the couch with the ice bag on his jaw, watching "Wheel of Fortune," Anastasia's favorite show, and groaning. He thought "Wheel of Fortune" was a really dumb show, and he *always* groaned when someone bought a vowel. "Why on earth does she waste money buying an E when she's already got T and H and *knows* the other letter's an E?" Myron Krupnik would say. And Anastasia would say "Shhhhh."

But on this particular night, Sam's dad had groaned because his mouth hurt.

Sam remembered it, but he couldn't see what it had to do with scary animal hats.

His mom explained. "Everybody has four wisdom teeth," she said, "way in the back."

"Me too?" Sam asked.

"Well, not yet. You'll get them when you're older, though. Everybody does. All grown-ups have four wisdom teeth."

Sam still couldn't see what it had to do with hats, but he kept listening. His mom handed him a cookie from the rack where they were cooling. He hoped it was one with a lot of raisins.

"And sometimes they have to be taken out. I had my wisdom teeth taken out when I was in college, actually."

"Did you have to have a bag of ice?"

"Yes, I did. I stayed overnight in the college infirmary."

Sam chewed on his cookie. "I don't want wisdom teeth," he told his mother. "I'm not going to have any."

"Well, Sam," his mom said, "the reason I asked if you remembered Daddy's wisdom teeth was this. He had four of them, and the dentist said they all had to come out. So he *could* have had them done one at a time. Maybe one each week."

"Then it wouldn't have hurt so much," Sam said.

"Well, maybe not. But it would have meant that every week he would have to think about it and worry about it. And then he would have one done, and it would get better, and he would have to start thinking about the *next* one."

"And you would have to make him four ice bags," Sam said.

"Right. But he decided to get it all over with at once. Your dad is a brave guy, Sam."

"Yeah." Sam chewed on his cookie and thought about his dad. He still couldn't figure out what this had to do with scary animal hats.

"So, here's my thought, Sam," his mother said. "You could just forget about those scary animal hats. You could forget about being a zooman. We could take that zooman suit and cut it up into rags and you would never have to wear it again. And we could throw the hats away."

Sam shook his head slowly. "No," he said. "I promised the other kids scary animals."

"I know you did. And I know you're a brave guy, too, like your dad." His mom hugged him, and he snuggled in her lap.

"Yes," Sam said. "I am." He tried to think about times when he had been brave. Once he had had to have a penicillin shot, and he hadn't cried.

"So it seems to me that you could do those — how many were there?"

"Five," Sam said.

"Yes, five. You could do those five hats one at a time, one each day, and you could drag it out and worry about it for five days. Or you could be like your dad and his wisdom teeth."

Now he saw what she meant. "And get them all over with at once!" Sam said.

"Right."

"Tomorrow," Sam said.

"All five?" his mom asked.

"All five," Sam said.

18

"Class," Sam announced, as he stood in front of the circle of children, "today will be a very special day."

"Where's your hat?" Leah asked.

"Hey! I can see Sam's hair!" Adam shouted.

Sam looked down at the plastic trash bag on the floor beside him. "I will be doing a lot of hats," he explained, "but I decided to do them one at a time instead of wearing them in a tower, the way I did birds. Remember I promised you scary animal hats? Today's the day."

"Uh, Sam," Mrs. Bennett asked politely, "how many will you be doing this morning? I had planned on a finger-painting project." She looked at her watch.

"Five," Sam told her.

"Goodness," Mrs. Bennett said, "I'm not sure we'll have time for five today, Sam."

"I have to," Sam said. "It's like wisdom teeth."

"Wisdom teeth?"

"These are five very scary animals," Sam explained.

"Do it, Sam! Do the scary ones!" Adam and some of the other boys began to call. "You promised really scary ones!"

Mrs. Bennett sighed. "Go ahead, Sam," she said.

Sam took the first hat out of the bag. He looked at it carefully to see which one it was, and then he put it on his head. "Big Ben?" he said. "Could you do the music from *Jaws?*"

Big Ben began to hum the scary music loudly. Some of the children joined in. Sam could see Becky cover her ears.

"I am now wearing my Sharks hat," Sam announced. "A zookeeper has to take care of sharks."

"Oh, *no!*" Becky moaned. She uncovered her ears and covered her eyes.

"But I know how to train sharks to behave,"

Sam explained. "Who would like to be a pretend shark?"

All of the boys waved their arms in the air, volunteering, and Sam chose Eli and Adam. "Swim toward me when I tell you to," Sam instructed them. "Not till I'm ready."

Eli and Adam lay on the carpet, waiting. They made their faces into scary faces, with their teeth showing.

"I have a special weapon," Sam explained. He reached into the bag and took it out.

"Sam," Mrs. Bennett said, in a warning sort of voice.

"It's not a gun," Sam reassured her. He turned toward the class and toward the two sharks who were waiting. "Okay, sharks," he said, *"swim."*

All of the children, led by Big Ben, were now humming the *Jaws* music loudly: all except Becky, who was curled in Miss Ruth's lap and had her face in her hands. Eli and Adam wiggled across the floor toward Sam.

It was very, very scary. Sam aimed his dog-training bottle of water with a teensy bit of vinegar and waited. When the two sharks were close enough, he shot them both.

"Yuck!" Eli and Adam jumped up, their faces

138

wet. The humming stopped. The shark attack was over.

"See?" Sam said. "It's easy to control sharks if you know what you're doing.

"Next," he said, changing his hat with a dramatic flourish, "I need a whole bunch of you to be a swarm of hornets!"

The class, all of them excited, began to buzz loudly. Leah began to move forward slowly in her wheelchair, and three others fluttered imaginary wings and aimed their stingers at Sam as they approached.

It was very, very scary. "Zzzzzzzzzzzzzzzzzzz," the class buzzed. But Sam, wearing his Hornets cap, tried to be as brave as the bravest possible zooman. He aimed his squirter, and one by one he shot the hornets and they dropped to the floor. Leah slumped over in her wheelchair, and said, "I'm dead. Zzzzz."

Sam changed hats again. "Now," he announced, "Grizzlies."

Big Ben got up from his seat. No one made a sound. There was no *Jaws* music, no zzzzzzz. There was just Big Ben, rising up into the silence with his arms raised high in the air and his fingers shaped into claws. He lurched forward slowly, moving his legs in huge thumps, growling. Then, suddenly, he began to give a terrible grizzly roar. It was the scariest thing Sam had ever seen, and it was coming right toward him.

He took aim and squirted Big Ben in the mouth, mid-roar.

The class cheered as the grizzly slowly slumped to the floor, defeated.

Sam took out another hat. This one scared him, but he wasn't entirely certain what it was. In the very beginning, when the hats were brand new, his mother had read each one to him, and he had set these five aside. His mom had agreed that this one was very scary, but she didn't know exactly what it was either.

"Devil rays," Sam announced in a loud voice. Everyone looked impressed and a little frightened, but no one said anything.

Becky uncovered her face. "That's a bad word," she said loudly, "and my mom says you shouldn't ever say it."

"Oh," Sam said. In his own house, there were certain bad words that you were not supposed to say. But *devil rays* was not one. "Well, I won't say it, then. Who would like to be —"

Becky interrupted him. She climbed off Miss Ruth's lap and stood with her hands on her hips. She stamped one foot. "I'm going to tell my mom if you keep wearing a hat with a bad word," Becky said in a loud voice.

Sam frowned. "Because of Becky, I'm going to take my Devil Rays hat off," he told the other children.

"And don't keep saying it, either," Becky insisted, "or I'll tell my mom."

Sam couldn't resist saying it again. "I wanted to tell you all about devil rays, class," he announced, "because I know you are very interested in devil rays, but I'm not going to, because of Becky, because Becky doesn't want me to say devil rays. I am now taking off my Devil Rays hat." Sam took off the cap and stuffed it back into the bag.

"You said the bad word four times," Becky pointed out.

Sam stared at her. "Make that five," he said defiantly. *"Devil rays."*

Becky flopped down on the floor to sulk.

"Now for the last one," Sam said. "I need long, skinny volunteers." Everybody looked at Miss Ruth, who was the longest and skinniest person

in the room. She laughed and raised her hand to volunteer. Lindsay and Peter joined her. "Okay," Sam said, "you need to lie on the floor and hiss."

The three volunteers lay on the carpet and made the sound "ssssssss."

Sam reached down into the bottom of the bag for his final scary hat. He put it on.

"Diamondbacks," he announced.

"Ooooh," said Mrs. Bennett. "That's a kind of rattlesnake!"

The hissing snakes wiggled toward Sam, flicking their tongues in a terrifying way. One by one Sam shot them with the squirter, and they quivered and lay still. The class applauded and cheered: all but Becky, who was still sulking.

"The end," Sam said triumphantly. He took off the Diamondbacks cap, put it into the bag, and bowed to the audience.

19

"Mrs. Bennett?" Sam went to stand beside his teacher as she was putting the jars of finger paint away in the supply closet.

"Yes, Sam?"

"I don't want to do hats anymore."

"That's okay, Sam," Mrs. Bennett said. "You've worked very hard at being a zooman for a lot of days now. You don't have to keep it up forever."

"I did all the best ones. There are only boring ones left, like broncos and marlins."

Mrs. Bennett knelt beside Sam. "I think actually you'd be wise to stop now because you did all the scary ones this morning and it was very exciting. Sometimes it's a good idea to stop at a

144

high point. Remember how you bowed and we all clapped? That was a good ending. You can take all those hats home and just store them away someplace."

"I'm tired of my hats," Sam whispered. "I don't even want to take them home." He glanced over at the fat trash bag sitting in a lumpy mound on the carpet beside the piano.

"How many did you say you had?"

"Thirty."

"I have an idea," Mrs. Bennett told Sam. "We have eighteen children in the school. And three teachers. That makes twenty-one. Shall we give everybody a hat?"

Sam nodded.

"And then shall we have a parade? I could play marching music on the piano, and we could all put on hats and march in a parade. We could use some exercise, I think."

Sam nodded eagerly.

Mrs. Bennett stood up, clapped her hands together to get the children's attention, and called, "Everybody! Let's get our paintings all rolled up! Sam has had a great idea!"

It had really been Mrs. Bennett's idea, Sam knew. But he liked that she said it was his. It made him feel important. He got the trash bag. And the children, with Miss Ruth's help, arranged themselves into a line.

While Sam was distributing hats, an absolutely amazing thing happened. It happened so sneakily, so quietly, that he almost didn't notice. But when he *did* notice, he was overwhelmed. He wanted to tell the whole world. But Sam decided he would tell his family first. He decided that he would *show* them. He would do it at dinner.

"Chief of Wonderfulness?" Sam's father asked. "Of course I understand. *Everybody* wants to become Chief of Wonderfulness, but for most of us it never happens. How did it happen to you?"

It was dinnertime. Every evening, at dinner, Sam's family talked about things that had happened during the day. Sam's things had always been small: maybe he had painted a good picture at school, or maybe he had visited Mrs. Stein next door, and she had given him a big glass of chocolate milk. Once Mr. Watson, the mailman, had let Sam walk with him and help deliver mail. Once Mr. Fosburgh, across the street, had called for help from his porch because his wheelchair was stuck, and Sam and

Anastasia had rescued him. All of those things were good things, but they were *small* good things.

But now, for the first time, something huge had happened. It was the most exciting day of Sam's life. It had made him into Chief of Wonderfulness at last, and he was trying to explain it to his family.

First he told them about the scary animal hats, and how the class had clapped and he had bowed at the end. Then he told about Mrs. Bennett's idea for the parade, and how he had stood by the bag and given each child a hat.

"And it was for keeps, too," Sam explained. "Not just for borrowing."

"Well, that was certainly generous of you, Sam," his mom said. "No wonder you felt wonderful. More potatoes, anyone?"

Sam sighed. He hadn't even gotten to the amazing part yet. Mrs. Krupnik spooned a second helping of mashed potatoes onto Anastasia's plate.

"Notice that Sleuth didn't even *budge* when you said 'potatoes,' Mom?" Anastasia asked. The dog, in his corner, looked up at the sound of his name.

"Or pork chops! I've said pork chops at least four times." Sleuth yawned at Mrs. Krupnik's voice and thumped his tail on the floor.

Sam clinked his fork against the side of his milk glass. That was how you got people's attention. "I'm not finished!" he said loudly.

"Not finished with your dinner, Sam?" his mom asked.

"No! With telling about what happened!"

"Oh, sweetie, I'm sorry. Please go on."

So Sam continued his description of the morning's events. "Everybody got in line, and they came up and said what hat they wanted, and I gave them the hat.

"Adam wanted Sharks, and I gave him Sharks.

"And Leah wanted Hornets, and I gave her Hornets.

"And Big Ben got Grizzlies.

"And dumb old Becky said she only wanted Bunnies or Kittens. So I gave her Devil Rays and *told* her it was Bunnies."

"Goodness," said Sam's mom, but he could see that she was smiling a little.

He could see, also, that they hadn't yet figured out the amazing thing.

"And after everybody had a hat but me, there were still some hats left," Sam explained.

"Which one did you want?" Anastasia asked.

"I didn't really want any one because I was tired of hats. But there was one at the bottom of the bag that I hadn't ever used because I didn't know what it said. It was sort of a mystery hat. And I decided to wear that one for the parade." Sam, telling them this part, began to get excited.

"A mystery hat. Sounds good," his dad said.

"So I took it out, and it wasn't a mystery hat anymore! It said PENGUINS!"

"Cool," Anastasia said. She passed her plate for more mashed potatoes. "I love penguins."

They didn't get it. Sam looked around at his family. They were each calmly eating. *They weren't getting it!*

"Excuse me, I'll be right back," Sam said. He climbed down from his chair, went into the study, to the special part of the bookcase, and found the book he wanted. He brought it back to the table.

"Look!" he said, and laid the book on the table with its cover facing up. *"Mr. Popper's Penguins."*

"One of your favorites," his father said. "Mine, too."

"The Arthur is Richard Atwater," Sam said, pointing to the cover.

"The author, Sam," his mother corrected gently.

"I know it's author. I just like to say Arthur. Excuse me again," Sam said, and ran back to the study. In a minute he had returned with an armload of books.

"Look," he said, and put another book on the table next to *Mr. Popper's Penguins.*

"Oh, cool," Anastasia said. *"The Great White Man-Eating Shark.* I love that one. It's really funny."

"Oh, I see, Sam! There are books about the same animals as your hats! Penguins, and now sharks. Isn't that interesting? Good for you, to figure that out!" Sam's mom smiled at him.

Sam opened *The Great White Man-Eating Shark.* "Listen," he said, and he began the story. "'There was once a boy named Norvin who was a good actor but rather plain. In fact, he looked very like a shark . . .'"

Mrs. Krupnik, leaning over to see the picture, laughed. "That *is* funny. What an odd-looking boy!"

Sam, exasperated, closed the book. He set another one on the table. *"Island Boy,"* he announced.

"She's a wonderful illustrator," Sam's mom said. She turned the pages of the book, looking at the colorful pictures of the island and the old-fashioned people.

Sam's dad was grinning. "Katherine," he said to Sam's mom, "you're not noticing something important."

"Well," Mrs. Krupnik said, still leafing through *Island Boy,* "there are so many details in these pictures that you have to look at each one very carefully."

"Try this one, Sam." His dad handed him one from the stack that he had set down on the floor.

Sam took the book. It was fatter than the others, more grown-up-looking. *"Harriet the Spy,"* Sam said.

"That used to be mine," Anastasia pointed out.

Sam turned to the first page. There were no pictures. "'Harriet was trying to explain to Sport how to play Town,'" the book began.

Sam looked up. His father was still grinning. Anastasia looked very surprised. And his mother, suddenly, was staring at him and had begun to cry a teeny bit. She dabbed at her eyes, and Sam could see that there were tears in them.

"Listen," Sam said proudly. He went to the corner of the kitchen where newspapers were stacked and ready to be taken out to the trash. He picked up a section of the *Boston Globe*.

"'Buffalo and Miami already have nine wins, and if the Oilers win one game, they'd bypass the Patriots as well,'" Sam said.

"And *now* listen," Sam said, putting the paper down. He picked up the cookbook that his mother had left on the counter beside the stove. He looked at the page, which had grease spatters on it. "'Pour off the fat from the skillet and sprinkle the chops with the carrots, onion, and garlic,'" Sam said.

Anastasia made a face. She looked at her plate in dismay. "Was there *garlic* in this?" she asked. "You know I hate garlic!"

"Sam!" said his mom, and held out her arms. "You can read!"

"Yes!" Sam said. "I'm the Chief of Wonderfulness!"

"I still want you and Dad to read me stories," Sam told his mom as she took him up the stairs to bed.

"Oh, of course," Mrs. Krupnik said. "We'll read you stories forever, if you let us. It's our favorite part of the day, when we read bedtime stories."

"And I can read them to you now, too," Sam pointed out.

"We can take turns, all four of us." His mom unzipped his zooman suit and helped him step out of it. "Boy," she said, "am I glad to get rid of this thing! Look: pork chop gravy on the sleeve." She dropped the zooman suit onto the floor beside his bed.

Sam stood still while she snapped his stars-and-planets pajamas. He looked down at the little heap of fleecy gray fabric on the floor, with its frayed cuffs and grape juice stains.

When his pajamas were all snapped, Sam leaned down and picked up the coverall. He ran his fingers over the red embroidered words that had made him into Zooman Sam. He remembered how, at the beginning — not that very long ago — his mother had had to help him sound out the word, putting together the zzz and the ooo and mmmm until he understood what it spelled. Now, magically, he could just look at it, and the word told itself to him. Not just the zooman word, but *all* words, even the hardest ones. He had read the title *Island Boy* just by looking at it, and "island" was a very hard word, with an "s" that you couldn't even hear.

He pulled at the end of the little red thread, and it began to unravel. The z disappeared.

"'Ooman Sam'" Sam read, and laughed aloud.

"Keep pulling," his mother told him. "It will all disappear and we can throw the zooman suit into the trash."

But Sam was looking at it. He was seeing something in his mind.

"Mom," he said, "see between the O and the M? There's a little bit of space there."

"Mmmmm," his mom replied. She was putting some clean clothes on his chair, for morning. Osh-Kosh overalls and a striped T-shirt. He hadn't worn such ordinary clothes in a long time.

"There's room for a whole other letter there," Sam said, still examining the place between the second O and the M. "You could put a K there."

"I could, but why would I?" his mother asked, with a puzzled look.

"Because," Sam said, feeling excited at his idea, feeling a whole new future starting, feeling the Chief of Wonderfulness feeling, "if you put a K there, and then you put a nice fat B at the beginning, you'd have a whole new word! You'd have a whole new *me!*"

He handed his mother the crumpled gray suit.

She stared at him, shaking her head. Then she smiled.

"Bookman Sam," she said.

"Bookman Sam," Sam repeated happily.

"Maybe I can get the gravy stains out," his mother said, and gave him a hug.